Ghost Town

Ghost Town

Tales of Manhattan Then and Now

Patrick McGrath

BLOOMSBURY

First published 2005

Copyright © 2005 by Patrick McGrath

The moral right of the author has been asserted

Bloomsbury Publishing Plc, 38 Soho Square, London WID 3HB

A CIP catalogue record for this book
is available from the British Library

10 9 8 7 6 5 4 3 2 1

ISBN 0 7475 7429 4

All papers used by Bloomsbury Publishing are natural,
recyclable products made from wood grown in well-managed
forests. The manufacturing processes conform to the
environmental regulations of the country of origin.

Typeset by Hewer Text UK Ltd, Edinburgh
Printed in Great Britain by Clays Ltd, St Ives plc

For Peter Carey;
and, as ever, for Maria

CONTENTS

THE YEAR OF THE GIBBET

I have been in the town, a disquieting experience, for New York has become a place not so much of death as of the *terror* of death. Many houses are deserted and from those which are not drift the fumes of preparations intended to protect the living still within. The streets are silent but for the faint wailing of the newly bereaved and the rumbling wheels of the melancholy death-carts hauling their loads to Potter's Field. In one square alone I saw five of them, each at a different door. Here and there can be glimpsed one of the few brave doctors who remain to minister to the sick. They hurry from house to house, the black bag in one hand and a camphor-rag in the other which they press to their faces to ward off the contagion. The docks are quiet. No shipping comes up from the Narrows now, indeed I have heard it said that New York is finished as a seaport, so vulnerable are we to disease, being a cross-roads for all the world. I see a skiff pushing off from the end of the wharf, a sail being run up, three children in the boat, two women, a few boxes. They are striking out for Long Island, intending to escape the contagion in those green fields. Vain hope, for wherever man goes, there goes the Pest—why flee? Better by far stay in one's own place, and there prepare for the end. That is my policy. It is the Fourth of July, 1832, fifty-five years since my mama died, and I have no doubt but that I will follow her before the week is out.

All my life I have lived in New York. I was too young properly to understand the events which preceded the Revolutionary War, but I can still recall an innocent time when Manhattan was a place of farms and tranquil orchards and it was said that visitors *smelled* the island even as their vessels came beating up through the Narrows, our wild-flowers and fruit trees.

At the southern tip sat the town itself, a trim assembly of step-gabled brick buildings on cobbled, shady, tree-lined streets, with roofs of tile and shingle painted every color under the sun. Deep-drafted trading vessels from all over the world docked at our wharves, our merchants prospered and with them a host of associated trades. My father was a cabinet maker who had steady work in the years of prosperity and only fell on hard times when the port was closed. Soon after that he enlisted in Washington's army and went north to join the troops besieging the British in occupied Boston.

Our house was on the west side of the town, on Lambert Street, behind the old Trinity Church—in the very *shadow* of Trinity, so it felt to me, for as a boy I liked to wander alone among the tilting gravestones which in places encroached upon the back garden where my mama grew vegetables and kept her chickens. I loved that house. My papa built it with his own hands and though I know it was a modest house, to the small boy I then was it seemed a mansion. To the north lay swampland and open fields with low bluffs hanging over the river and oyster boats pulled up on the banks below. Cattle grazed in the pastures above Warren Street, and in summer the grass grew as high as a man's waist. To the south lay the harbor, and often I crossed the island with my mama to watch the big ships come to their mooring at the East River wharves.

From an early age I was taught by my mama to regard the British as cunning tyrants whose sole design was to abase and enslave the American people. Lately, in moments of nocturnal sentiment, in back of some South Street grog shop, and disguised in liquor, I can still regard the Revolution as a struggle in which the cause prevailed because our destiny demanded that it do so; our *destiny*, yes. Though in the chill light of dawn that follows my illusions fade like a mist off the harbor and I remember a quite different narrative, one far darker. For the Revolutionary War was a time of horror and I for one recall those days not with pride but with an abiding sense of shame.

In the spring of '76, when I was ten, it became known that the enemy had evacuated Boston and put out to sea. Washington's soldiers, my father among them, came streaming back into New York and at once set about tearing up the cobblestones and digging ditches in the streets. Our trees were cut down for barricades and cannon were mounted on every promontory which overlooked the water. Soon the town more resembled a fortified camp than a thriving

Atlantic seaport. For some time our trade had been shut down, and the mud in the docks gave off horrid vapors at low water, this in addition to the unwholesome stinks from so many people in so small a compass all packed together like herrings in a barrel, many diseased with the Itch, the Pox, the Flux, what have you—the town now stank.

The world was turned upside down.

Their fleet arrived at the end of June and dropped anchor in the Lower Bay. We climbed to the top of Pitt Hill, I remember, and I was awed at the sight of so many ships together, all that white sailcloth billowing in the sunshine and their masts as thick as trees in a wood. But I damn near fouled my britches when my brother Dan told me they were King George's ships and had come with their cannon to blow us all to smithereens!

And yet for weeks they did nothing. They settled themselves on Staten Island and we waited to see what they would do next. Then at last came news: we heard that they had crossed to Long Island. That was where Washington fought them. He was badly beaten and lost many men. The next morning as we sat at our breakfast in a silent, fearful house, in limped my father with his pack and musket. He was a small, troubled man, my papa, and that day his troubles were great. He was unshaven and dirty, his clothes were torn, and his head was bound with a blood-stained bandage. He told us they had been surrounded by the enemy and many died as they tried to get away. Some were drowned in the swamps along Gowanus Creek and some who wanted to surrender were stuck through with bayonets. He said he saw men clutching their bellies to keep their innards from spilling out, others collapsing from loss of blood and drowning in a few feet of water as their friends rushed past them, not pausing in their panic. It was a bloody massacre, he said. Those lucky enough to escape pitched up on the high ground just back of Brooklyn village and entrenched themselves as best they could.

All this he told us as he sat at the kitchen table barely touching the plate of food my mother had put before him. Then had come a storm, he whispered. The thunder and lightning was dreadful, and we were soaked to the bone. That night the two armies could not see each other though camped not a hundred rods apart. We were trapped, he said, what was left of us, up there on Brooklyn Heights. Nothing for it but to surrender.

He wiped his mouth with his sleeve and looked at us, nodding. He drank off some ale.

—So what happened? said my brother Daniel.

—What happened? He saved us.

—Who?

Who? Even I knew who!

—Most of us was ferried across in the night. The last came over at daybreak, and the General the last of all. If we hadn't got away it would all be over for us, and Washington's head in a noose.

—In a *noose*!

I was shocked, this I do remember, at the thought of General Washington with his head in a noose.

So now with rumors flying that the redcoats would soon come ashore at Kips Bay our men were retreating up the west side of the island in hopes of holding them off at Harlem Heights. We all cheered when my mother kissed our frightened papa at the back door, then took his shaggy head in her fingers and told him that when he came back she would be waiting for him. She turned away, wiping at a fugitive teardrop, and then he was gone. That was the last I saw of him.

My mama was the only safe and stable element in this upside-down world. She worked from dawn to dusk. She made soap, she wove cloth, she dipped candles. She grew fruit, she fattened pigs and chicken for the table, and gave birth to child after child though only three of us survived infancy, of whom I was her favorite, being the small, sickly one. I believe she thought she might not have me for long. She was a proud, strong woman—the way she argued with my papa, prodding his chest, and him a man of at times violent temper—especially when in drink—but she never yielded an inch. She was obstinate and blunt-spoken, and fiercely protective of her own, a big, handsome woman with broad shoulders and a thrusting chin, her neck a column of flesh the color of marble—

But let me not speak of her neck.

Before me on the table now I have her skull. It is curiously modest in scale, though in life it appeared large, for a great mass of auburn hair was pinned atop it in an untidy bun from which strands drifted loose as she moved about her kitchen and her garden. She was a true patriot and I never once saw her fearful, as I had seen my poor papa. None was more ardent in their devotion to the republic, nor did she lose heart as so many did when New York was invaded. She worked for the cause from within the occupied town and her flame burned bright even if it burned but briefly before being snuffed out like a guttering candle.

As for my papa, it is hard for me to provide any more distinct picture of him beyond what I remember of him that last breakfast he ate with us after the Battle of Brooklyn. He perished at Valley Forge. He died of a malignant bilious fever contracted from sleeping in dirty blankets. But though I barely knew the man, I revere his memory. Each year I drink a glass of wine in the observance of the anniversary of his death.

I have drunk the last, God help me.

When the bombardment began—two weeks after that last breakfast with my poor papa— my mother led my brother Dan, my sister Lizzie, and me along the familiar path through the graveyard and down a flight of old stone steps into the Trinity vaults, where we found our neighbors taking shelter. In a state of acute distress I sat in the gloom and listened to the muffled roar from the warships in the East River. Every explosion startled and terrified me. I was sure the roof would at any moment fall in. The vaults were cold and my nostrils soon filled with the fetid smell which issued from the tombs all around.

My mama sat in the shadows with her back straight and her head held high, her hands clamped tight upon her knees and her expression grim and unchanging. She said nothing. I buried my face in her skirts, and absently she stroked my head. I was shuddering, I remember, and sobbing in my terror. I begged her to take me out of that stinking place but she only put her finger to my lips. I stared at the roof of the vault as though I would learn there the extent of the devastation being wrought above our heads—cannonballs hissing through the streets, bouncing off walls, smashing into buildings and cellars—thick smoke drifting over the houses, shells whistling in the air—muskets cracking—

Even as I sit here some fifty years later, pen uplifted, high above the death-carts and the quicklime, I am yet again roused to a tired rage at the memory of what was done to us. It is a backward-looking rage, for I was a child and did not altogether comprehend the enormity of the insult. After the bombardment the town was much changed: buildings smashed up, many still burning, soldiers everywhere, and people taking to the streets to welcome them, the fools—they made of it a carnival!

I was on Broadway with my sister Lizzie the next day, walking down through the destruction to the harbor when all at once a troop of redcoats emerged from a side street and came toward us at the run. Sunlight gleamed on their bayonets like sheets of fire and the dust rose in clouds beneath their feet. At the head of the column rode a stout man with a large curved nose which resembled the blade of a scythe. He was mounted on a tall bay mare, and though I had seen plenty of English gentlemen on the streets of New York, and not a few officers, somehow he was not like any of them. His skin was white as chalk and his lips were scarlet and he wore a plumed silver helmet and a pale blue coat edged with gold. As he rode by I saw how he sat his horse with the reins held limp in his fingers as though he were in a chair in a drawing room making conversation to a lady, indeed he *rode* like a lady, and on his plump face played a haughty smile as he glanced down at the cheering townspeople.

I ran home and told my mama about the painted officer with the hook nose and the feathers who rode like a lady and acted like a king. There were other women in the kitchen and they looked at one another, lifting their eyebrows and nodding. My mama was gutting a fish. She sniffed with contempt.

—Lord John Hyde, she said, wiping the slime from her hands. She sat down and stood me in front of her and put her hands on my shoulders. All at once this was serious.

—Did he speak to you, little one?

—No, mama.

—Good boy. Stay clear of him, do you understand me?

The other women murmured their agreement.

—Yes, mama.

As I turn her poor skull in my fingers now a strange heat rises within me, and I plant my lips briefly upon her cranium, which is yellowed, and beginning to reveal a fine network of tiny cracks. I set it back down upon the table and take up my pen once more. I am not known as a man of unswerving sobriety but I do not exaggerate when I say that what befell us next was a thousand times worse than anything that had thus far occurred.

* * *

Late one night barely a week after the occupation began, a fire started in a tavern on Whitehall Slip, set by an American incendiary, it was said, who was following Washington's secret order that the enemy be denied winter quarters in New York. The identity of that incendiary has never been established. There have been rumors over the years, many of which point to an American sea captain named Miles Walsh who caused great trouble to the British on several occasions. I remember my mama coming into our bedroom in the middle of the night and telling us to get dressed for the town was ablaze.

Then I was outside buttoning my britches and staring at the sky over the Battery which was lit by a furious red glow. All was heat and smoke. People were shouting, dogs howling, figures running to and fro, and though the fire was still some way off I could hear buildings falling and the roaring of flames. We joined the crowd moving north on Broadway. The night was pierced by the screams of women, and wind-blown embers and scraps of burning cloth and paper floated about me in the darkness. I was bewildered and afraid and then I heard my mama cry out. When I turned I saw that Trinity was blazing like a fired ship, ghostly black ribs of beam and rafter for a second visible within the flames before being engulfed once more.

Then with a great crash the roof fell in and moments later the steeple came down after it in a fountain of fire.

The blaze cut a swath from Whitehall up the west side to the grounds of King's College, where it died for lack of fresh buildings to consume. No surprise that men wept and some were driven beyond weeping: for having first been turned into a fortified camp, then bombarded for days by cannon, then invaded by the British, the town now lay devastated by fire. If it *was* Miles Walsh who started it, then for all his revolutionary ardor he did no good to the people of New York that night. For in this wrecked and smoking place, in this *ruin*, there was no glory, no victory, only suffering.

I do not know where we slept that night. We made a sorry sight, I am sure, at dawn, the crowd tramping homeward but without homes to go to. It was into a wasteland that we returned. Where once stood houses and orchards there was now no more than a smoking tract of black earth with here and there fragments of chimneys and parts of walls. Families knelt in prayer, others stood in silent shock or picked among the ashes attempting to recover what was left of their property. I saw bodies burned almost beyond recognition and they haunted my dreams for many months after.

Down Broadway we shuffled through this spectacle of desolation. Dan was silent, his expression one of anger and bewilderment while Lizzie was as distressed as I had ever seen her, careless even that her dress was trailing in the ashes. My mother showed only the thin grim line of mouth which I knew well, that way she had of clamping her out-thrust jaw so tight the sinew in her neck stood up, and her eyes ablaze as fierce as anything I saw the night before. Her hair was wild and she pushed it back unaware of what she was doing, and her face became blackened with soot.

Of Trinity Church all that remained were ruined walls. Smoking beams lay tumbled upon one another and in the churchyard the headstones were charred, many of them cracked and split or fallen over in pieces, leaving only a snagged fraction like the remnant of a rotted tooth. A part of our own chimney still stood, being made of brick, the stump of it but nothing else. Nor were we the only ones. Almost every house west of Broadway was gone. We stood with the few pitiful possessions we had carried away in the night and stared at the burnt ground where our house had once been. I looked up at my mama and all at once her eyes filled with tears, though none spilled down her face. She shook her head, she could not speak. It was Lizzie who finally broke the silence.

—Where are we to go, mama?

And then our mama showed her mettle. Her shoulders heaved, she lifted a fist. She said again what she had said when Howe's fleet dropped anchor in the Lower Bay. Many of our neighbors had packed up and gone but not us, oh no, we did not flee, my mother was having none of *that*! She had relations in Jersey but she had quarreled with them years before. She declared she would rather fight the British with her bare hands than go creeping to her people at the first sign of trouble.

—Where are we to go, she said. Where should we go, Lizzie? There is nowhere for us to go but here!

And it was then that we heard from somewhere behind us a bark of laughter. Above the slow-moving tide of homeless people streaming down Broadway sat a lone, plumed horseman on a tall bay mare.

All that I have suffered this last fifty years has its beginning in what next occurred. The Englishman's horse picked its way down past the ruins and into the scorched trees of the graveyard. Lord John Hyde sat swaying in the saddle, and I realized only later that he was drunk, having come, it may be, from some convivial gathering of his fellow officers after the excitement of the night before. My mama did not hesitate. She strode up through the headstones to where the horse pawed the earth among the blackened tree-trunks. I remember thinking how brave she was to be challenging this proud officer atop his huge animal, for he certainly terrified me. Trails of smoke and occasional spurts of flame arose from heaps of smoldering wood scattered about the graveyard, and horse and rider appeared to shimmer like a visitation from out of a romance. Our neighbors gathered about us, drawn by this plumed and swaying horseman come to inspect us in our loss and my mama standing there before him. His drawling voice carried clear in the damp heavy air of the morning.

—Now, madam, you see what happens to those who will not pay their taxes!

And with that he turned and began making his way back up toward the road, small clouds of ash rising under his horse's hooves.

—Will you not help us, Lord Hyde?

But he said nothing more, merely flicked at the horse with his whip. My mama could take no more. It all burst out of her.

—You painted whore! she shouted. You king's strumpet!

Suddenly all was still. I felt the first drops of rain. Slowly Lord Hyde turned his horse. My mama did not move. She set her fists upon her hips and tossed her head as the rain began to fall. He lifted his whip. All at once I saw that he would come down upon her, that he would *ride her down* and whip her as she lay trampled and screaming in the ashes—

But it did not happen. He stared at her a second as though to fix her in his mind and then turned once more. He spurred the horse back up on to Broadway, where the people fell back as he cantered away. It began to rain in earnest then, and the ashes hissed and smoked all around us.

*   *   *

Strange to say, the encounter with Lord Hyde roused my mother from the shock of the destruction of our home, and now that she saw what must be done it was to my brother Dan that she turned.

Dan was a boy of fourteen who in many ways resembled my papa. He had been apprenticed to a carpenter, being suited like my papa to work with his hands. He was even then assailed by inner troubles and mysteries, a tortured boy. In later years he suffered various disasters and took to drink, and died a bitter, disappointed man. I buried him one winter in Trinity graveyard and myself wrote the death notice. But now his hour was come. He stood listening to my mama, she with her homespun shawl fluttering about her shoulders, and him in his tattered shirt and britches. There they were, mother and son, speaking low to each other as they gazed out over the black barren earth and the Hudson lapping at the bluffs beyond, and it is extraordinary to me that a woman who had lost everything in a fire and with no husband at her side could inspire her boy to construct a shelter for her. How Dan did it I do not well remember but in the space of a day and with the help of our neighbors a shack was framed with timbers from the roof of Trinity and covered with sailcloth begged and stolen from the East River wharves. Even Lizzie helped, for I can see her now with a flathead nail between her lips as she hammered a length of flapping canvas to a plank.

It was the first of the shelters to be built after the fire of '76. By nightfall many of those who now owned nothing but the clothes on their backs were settled inside it. Their eyes gleamed from every corner of the squat rough shack. My mama sat by the fire with a cup of rum, elbows on her knees and legs wide apart, smoking her old clay pipe and telling us that when the war was over we would remember with pride the day we built ourselves a house. She said it was the first step in building ourselves a nation.

In the weeks that followed other women followed my mama's example and set their children to work. Shacks and cabins began to rise across the bare earth behind the ruins of Trinity Church. So was born a new settlement. It became known as Canvas Town.

Canvas Town. Soon enough it was a place of debauchery, violence, chicanery—the new nation indeed! It was late fall now. Winter was approaching. Strong winds blew from the harbor, and large chunks of ice drifted down the Hudson. The river began to freeze over. Wood and grain were scarce and of meat and poultry there was almost none, for New York had become a military garrison. What supplies came in from the farms of Long Island were taken by the British, and whatever went to market was priced too high for the residents of Canvas Town. Meanwhile the streets and canals ran with the enemy's filth, and wharves where once the merchant ships of the world had docked began to sag and rot with neglect, and at low tide the East River was a murky sheet of sewage. The town stank worse than ever.

As winter came on, the hardships of life in Canvas Town began truly to bite. I was profoundly miserable for I hated having to crawl each night into a narrow wooden box that smelled of fish. My mama said there were many in New York who would be happy of a fish-box to sleep in. I said I was not one of them and she laughed, then sat me in her lap and pressed me to her bosom. Murmuring loving words, she stroked my head. She was a strong presence in our fledgling settlement but by degrees, as the weather grew colder, her spirits weakened and a darkness at times stole over her. On hearing of some new piece of infamy on the part of the British she would not rage as once she had but sink, rather, into silence. In answer to my anxious inquiry she would say only that she did not see what was to be done.

—I am of no use to my country, she whispered.

—But mama, will they not sail away when General Washington has beat them?

—They will never sail away! she cried.

Nor could we ever forget that we lived under martial law, if law it could be called. At the top of the Common stood the Provost, most abhorred of all the prisons in the town, with the gibbet out front where American soldiers were hanged in plain view and left there for days so that nobody could forget the penalty for rebellion. Other hangings occurred at dead of night on Barrack Street and of those we were supposed to know nothing, although of course we did. They moored hulks in the East River and sent our soldiers to rot in their holds. The stink of those foul prison-ships carried clear across to Manhattan, as did the ghastly moans and cries of men and women condemned to perish within them. Dead soldiers lay among the living and the cold was so bad and the men so weak their limbs blackened and went bad with the gangrene. Those who survived were starved close to death then fed poisoned bread, and their corpses were tossed overboard in filthy shrouds like so much garbage.

These stories made a profound impression upon me. I grew mortally terrified of being cast into one of the British prisons on the island.

In the midst of all this suffering, British officers caroused in mansions once the property of American merchants. It was a winter of constant festivity for Lord John Hyde and his friends, of balls and banquets where sauced meats were savored and fine wines drunk. Plays were put on in the theaters and gentlemen gambled for high stakes at cards, and in elegant drawing rooms musicians in powdered wigs and silk stockings performed chamber pieces for ladies in glittering gowns. The whores did fine trade, many having premises in the vicinity of the Trinity ruins, and by night the town was raucous with the cries of drunken Englishmen howling for females like apes.

Thus the army of occupation. See what we had by contrast. We struggled daily to secure the wherewithal to keep body and soul together and lived hopeless lives in low hovels amid the mud and filth of Canvas Town. Ragged and emaciated, we haunted the streets like the living dead, standing on bread lines, grubbing for bones, and many indeed did perish of cold and hunger and disease, though not so many as died of deliberate neglect in the East River prison-hulks. My mama lay on her straw mattress and stared at the roof. The canvas was stained now and stitched and patched where it had split open. I crawled close so as to share the warmth of her body, and at these times an animal somnolence would settle on the shack.

Then one morning I awoke in my box to see a stranger stooped in the doorway. For some seconds I did not know if I was dreaming. He was a tall man with a red beard and a thin, sharp face. He was dressed like a Quaker in a shabby black coat and britches and he was clutching a wide-brimmed black hat in his hand, also a long stick with a brass knob at one end. He held back the blanket which hung on the inside of the door and quietly spoke my mama's name. She struggled awake then sat up at once.

—Miles Walsh, she murmured, hitching her shawl about her bosom.

The foxy man stooped low and stepped inside and the blanket swung to behind him. Other bodies stirred into wakefulness. Always the shack was crowded at night. With her shawl wrapped tight about her my mama knelt at the hearth and roused the embers of the fire. Miles Walsh sat down on a box, his knees jutting out sharply on either side of his brass-knobbed stick, upon which he folded his long thin fingers, and upon them set his whiskered chin: this the man who burned down half of New York, though at the time I had no inkling of that. Quickly, I was sent out to keep watch. I was to tell my mama at once if there were redcoats about. Some time later she emerged from the shack with this Miles Walsh and told me we were going to the seaport.

We crossed the town by way of the twisty back streets where we would be unlikely to encounter a patrol. We passed crudely erected market stalls where the poor purchased what they could of those overpriced commodities not already commandeered by the army of occupation. A light rain was falling, the day was misty and from the harbor came the screech of seagulls. There was a smell of fish in the air and a tart smack of salt. They walked fast and I had to run to keep up. My mama wore her shawl about her head like a cowl, and her skirt as it swept through the puddles became spattered with mud. The shops and houses of merchants were shuttered, many of them, or else occupied by loyalist families who had sought protection within the garrison New York had become.

Close to the river we slipped down an alley which gave on to the deserted back yard of a seaman's tavern called the Rising Sun. Barrels were stacked precariously against a brick wall and to one side stood a large cart. Miles Walsh had us wait by the gate then crossed the yard in a few strides. Glancing about him he then darted up a wooden staircase fastened to the outside of the back of the building. Close to the roof was a small door with an iron hook set in the brick from which dangled a length of chain. There he paused and again looked about, a curious figure high up against the bricks that misty morning.

A few minutes later we were standing all three in a narrow wooden gallery on the top floor of the tavern. I felt sick to be so high and with so little between me and the nothingness on the other side of a flimsy balustrade which overhung a drinking hall three floors below. Beneath us, several dozen men sat at rough tables or leaned against a counter that ran the length of the room. Redcoats stood drinking with the rest and there arose to my senses a din of human voices, a quantity of tobacco smoke and a strong smell of ale. Miles Walsh put his hands on his knees and leaned down to speak to me.

—Stay here, boy, he said, and if they come up the stairs you find me.

He meant the redcoats. For more than an hour I sat there in mortal fear of my life. I could not look down through the haze of smoke upon the drinkers below even if by my weakness I put my mama at risk. I had never encountered this Miles Walsh before but it was clear that he and my mama had secret business to conduct and that it must be done without knowledge of the British for it was certainly to do with some action *against* them. This made me greatly uneasy. I did not want to think of my mama being thrown in prison. What then would become of me?

Thus my childish thinking as I sat shivering with terror high in the gallery above the drinkers. I was growing sleepy when I heard voices down the corridor and saw Miles Walsh, followed by my mama and three others. Two were seafaring men in canvas trousers, each with a pigtail and tattoos inked upon his skin. The third was a man in his middle years in a good suit of clothes and wearing a cocked hat with scarlet trim, a man of some standing and authority, a merchant, perhaps, or a shipowner. I did not like any of them. I wanted to take my mama away from there.

When we were in the yard behind the tavern Miles Walsh turned to me and told me I had done well. He told me to say nothing of the work I had done and I should have more of it. Then he gave me a penny. Thus was I recruited, and thus would I be ruined: for a penny. My mama and I returned to Canvas Town by the alleys and back streets and encountered no soldiers. When we were once more safe at home my mama told me I was to be her eyes and ears, this was my work now. I was to look out for her wherever we went.

I did not tell her that I had not been her eyes in the Rising Sun. I had been too frightened to watch the soldiers in the hall below.

—Who are those men, mama? I said.

—They are friends, she said. Friends of America.

* * *

My hand trembles as I lift the glass to my lips. It is white rum from the sugar islands that I favor these days, it seems to spill at least a little sunlight into this dark constricted cell I call my soul. The silence unsettles me. Never have I known a Fourth of July so quiet as this one. We knew the pestilence was coming, of course. We knew its path lay to the west, and that having ravaged Europe it would find its way across the Atlantic. Everything finds its way across the Atlantic in the end. If our Pilgrim Fathers believed they had left the corruption of old Europe behind them, how wrong they have been proven! The corruption of old Europe— why, they brought it with them, it came ashore at Plymouth Rock! I think in my mother's day we saw the last American effort to cleanse ourselves of the stain of old Europe; certainly it was in this spirit that she fought and died for the republic.

All over town the living continue to sicken and anyone with dollars enough to remove to the countryside has done so by stagecoach or steamboat or wheelbarrow or even on foot, which is the reason for the silence attending this anniversary of the Declaration of our In-dependence. I am going nowhere. I have not the means to remove myself nor have I anywhere to go to. And like my mother I am loath to flee the town at the first sign of trouble. It will kill me, of course, New York will kill me, but better by far to perish here alone in my garret than take my chance on the high road and finish my days in some alien pesthouse or a ditch. No, I will go down, as they say in the grog shops hereabouts, with my *vessel*! With my *ship*! I am avoiding the town pumps and dosing myself with rum instead, but it is only a matter of time before the black vomit comes. The doctor as good as told me so when he visited me earlier. He did not say it in so many words but I caught the sour twitch of his lip when he turned his back on me and busied himself with his little black bag: a death sentence. I live too close to the river, he said. The pestilence that walketh in darkness, he said— for so it is called by our preachers—prefers to travel by water. What a wag.

I was perhaps too liberal with my medicine and have had to sleep an hour. Now I take up my pen once more with this purpose only—this *imperative*—which is to tell the true circumstance of my mother's last days. Few are aware of what she suffered at the hands of Lord John

Hyde and fewer still of my own part in the
events which precipitated her end. 1777 had
dawned upon a people plagued with doubt and
apprehension. The Year of the Gibbet: those
three grim sevens, an invisible noose dangling
from each of their crossbars, and a busy year for
the gibbet it would prove to be. I was with my
mama when they took her on the Hudson pier
and later discovered incriminating letters on her
person. They were addressed to that certain
gentleman I saw on the top floor of the Rising
Sun and they came from General Washington
himself. It seems that they involved the firing of
British ships in New York harbor.

I cannot say I was surprised. There had been a
second journey to the seaport. It was an over-
cast day and I stood with my mama on the
windy wharf as the intrepid revolutionary with
his collar turned up and his Quaker hat pulled
low indicated with small quick gestures certain
of the vessels riding at anchor offshore. There
was talk among them about winds and tides,
fireboats and gunpowder, and men whose
names meant nothing to me. I remember glancing about as I had been told to do and seeing
two British naval officers approaching. At once
I touched my mother's sleeve. In a second the

conversation turned to the price of cheese and continued in this vein until the danger was past, at which time it returned to the fiery destruction of shipping and the conditions in which this might best be accomplished.

These were large matters and required communication with General Washington. It became my mama's part in the affair to take regular journeys across the Hudson and into the Jerseys. It was understood that a woman could cross the British lines with far greater ease than a man and that this was how messages might be passed between the General and his conspirators in the town.

I well remember the first of those journeys and my surprise at what I saw. The given reason for it—the reason, that is, which my mama provided a certain army captain who signed her pass, was that she and her son needed to visit her relations in Newark. Of course we never once visited my mama's relations. Instead we took the Morristown road and traveled to the American camp, where my mama retired into a tent with an officer called Tallmadge and I was left to wander by myself.

I knew the trim tents and well-stocked barracks of the British troops in New York and had thought that our soldiers would be housed in similar fashion. But no. Ragged, bearded men, many of them barefoot, sat about campfires with blackened pots in the embers and gazed at me with incurious eyes. A few called out to me but with no real conviction. They were too cold, too dispirited and hungry to show more than a flickering interest in an unfamiliar child. I thought again of the soldiers I saw every day in New York and wondered why they did not cross the river and fall upon these poor weak men and massacre them as they had massacred so many at the Battle of Brooklyn.

We made the return journey to New York the following day, carrying with us a small sack of rice and a basket of vegetables. As soon as we got back to Canvas Town we were visited by Miles Walsh. My mama took him into the shack, in which by now were hidden arms and ammunition of various sorts, also handbills and other documents related to the patriot cause. They talked in low voices while I stood guard in the cold rain outside. We made four such journeys and on those days when we were not traveling my mama sent Lizzie and me to the seaport to count the ships lying at anchor there. We were to remember the nature of the cargoes we saw being unloaded and listen to any conversation on which we could eavesdrop without arousing suspicion. Most important, we were to tell her if we saw red-coats being embarked for a voyage, and if so, how many. For what Washington most feared was a fleet sailing out of New York harbor and up the Hudson, so as to sever New England from the other colonies. Then like a cleft skull the country would be split into two parts and the war would be lost.

I have come to believe that women are better suited to espionage than men. Certainly Lizzie took pleasure in asking the soldiers subtle questions cleverly disguised as feminine witter. She would carry the information back to Miles Walsh and glow with pride when he thanked her for her work. I wanted no part of any of it. But my mama needed my help and I did not know how to refuse her.

It is with the most profound remorse that I remember our last journey together. Lizzie was with us and we set off at dawn one cold clear morning and crossed to the Jersey shore, having passed the sentry at the Hudson pier without difficulty. The day was dry and we made good time to Newark and then we were on the Morristown road. We were carried for some miles in the back of a farm wagon loaded with sacks of potatoes bound for the American camp. The sky became cloudy late in the morning and soon we felt the first drops of rain. It seemed we were in for a soaking. We passed through a desolate stretch of country with wooded hills to either side of the road and no human habitation to be seen. Lizzie was made uneasy by the emptiness of the landscape and chattered away about nothing but my mama sat quite silent, wrapped in her shawl, her legs drawn up and her arms around her knees with her back against the potato sacks.

Then all at once we heard horses approaching. Leaping up, I saw a group of uniformed men come cantering down the road toward us. My mama did not move. She asked were they American troopers and I said I thought they were. We were each then taken up on a trooper's horse and set off west toward Morristown, leaving the potato wagon far behind us as the rain began to come down. Never had we had such an escort before. Lizzie's temper was much improved despite the weather. Thirty minutes later we rode into the American camp, where my mama was at once taken to the tent of General Washington himself.

When we left the next day once more we rode with the troopers. They brought us down to within a few miles of the ferry landing on the Jersey shore. It was a cold, raw day, I remember, and my mama was silent. It was clear to me that something of far greater import than usual had occurred and that it was to do with her conversation with General Washington. But she did not speak of it. I felt sure that some momentous action was imminent. Perhaps that very night, I thought, I should again see a great conflagration, but this time in the harbor, with shuddering explosions and ships afire with blazing spars and sails of flame and burning British sailors leaping screaming into the water—!

It was afternoon when we climbed on to the pier on the Manhattan shore. There we were met by the army captain who had issued my mama her pass, also three redcoats. My mama produced from within her clothing a crumpled sheet of paper which she then unfolded and pointed to his own scrawled signature. He asked her why we had traveled to Newark and she replied, as she always did, that we had been to visit her sister's family, for her mother was in poor health.

The captain stared at the pass once more. We stood at the end of the pier with our basket of vegetables, shivering in the damp wind coming off the harbor. Never before had our pass been scrutinized with such close attention. I tried not to show my anxiety though I know now that by the very effort I revealed much. But I was a child! What did they expect of me? All at once the officer turned to me and spoke in a loud voice.

—Boy, is this true?

I looked at my mama and for a moment I was brave.

—Yes, sir, I said.

He stared hard at me.

—Tell me what is wrong with your grandmother.

I said nothing. The captain sank down so his eyes were on a level with mine.

—What is your name? he said.

—Edmund.

—What is wrong with your grandmother, Edmund? You have just visited her in Newark, have you not?

I was not brave anymore, I was confused and frightened by this loud man with his fierce blue eyes! All I could think was that if I told him a lie he would lock me up in a dark stinking hole without my mama. I covered my mouth with my hand and as I did so I saw something flare in his eyes. He stood up. My mama stepped between us. She pushed me behind her and drew close to the officer.

—You are frightening the child, she said quietly. He does not trust you. We have had a long journey, sir. We want to go home.

But no, he would not let us go home, and now Lizzie realized the gravity of our situation. We were to go with him; and not an hour has passed from that day to this that I have not been tormented with the thought that it was *all my fault*—that it was my behavior on the dock that day which aroused the officer's suspicion, and set in motion my mama's destruction—

And the tapping at my door starts up again as it does whenever this idea begins to circle in my mind, and try as I might I cannot ignore it but must cross the room and find *again* that nobody is there, unless of course it is Death himself who comes knocking, and given that the cholera encroaches even now, his presence would be no surprise. Indeed, it would be welcome.

*   *   *

We sat on a hard bench in the back of a wagon and the captain escorted us on horseback. My poor mama, she showed nothing, but what torment she must have suffered as we were carried toward Lord Hyde's headquarters. Lizzie too was silent, and threw worried glances at my mama, who reached for her hand and pressed it. Our road passed to the north of Barrack Street, which is now called Chambers, and then across the island to Kips Bay. After what seemed an interminable journey through a landscape of empty fields and leafless trees, and steep hills with fast-running streams between, in the late afternoon we approached a mansion built of red brick that was partly hidden by a high stone wall into which were set a pair of iron gates. Once the property of a wealthy merchant of republican sympathies it was now the headquarters of Lord John Hyde.

The attempt to forget the wrong that man did my mother has kept me in the grog shops of the seaport this past fifty years. When he entered the room to which we had been taken, some sort of pantry, I believe, his manner was more sober than I had thus far seen it in my two passing glimpses of the man. He stood looking my mama up and down and I knew her insult still rankled in him. He then turned to the captain with a lifted eyebrow. He seated himself at the table in the middle of the room. It was very cold in there. The floor was of stone, the walls of whitewashed plaster, and there was a single window which looked out onto the courtyard at the back of the house. Several panes of glass were missing.

—You have a choice, madam, said Lord Hyde.

He pulled on a close-fitting glove of soft white leather.

—I intend to search you, and you will first undress yourself, or you will be undressed by others.

He was speaking to my *mother*! I turned to Lizzie and saw the color rise in her cheeks.

—You sons-of-bitches, said my mama—or spat, rather.

—Choose.

Lizzie and I had by this time been brought behind Lord Hyde's chair, so my mama stood alone. She did not hesitate. I watched her drop her shawl to the floor and then begin to remove her outer garments. There were men's faces pressed to the window and through the broken pane I saw them grinning. She stood against the wall in only her linen. Her undergarments were not clean, nothing could be kept clean in Canvas Town. For a moment there was silence. Then Lord Hyde spoke again.

—Undress, madam.

A profound shame swept over me. That this should be happening to my *mama*, and in front of all these strangers, these *Englishmen*—! Then with dawning wonder I realized that in her pride my mama *refused* shame! Again I glanced at my sister and she too had seen it. Our mama seemed to say, as she removed her soiled undergarments, that they mattered nothing, these rags, what mattered lay deeper, and of that Lord Hyde could not strip her. I stared at the floor but no sooner had I done so than the portly lord turned in his chair.

—Lift your head, boy, he whispered.

I did nothing.

—*Lift your head.*

There was that in his tone which commanded obedience. I had not the strength to defy him. I lifted my head. My mama stood naked against the whitewashed wall. Never had I seen her so, not even in the close confines of our crowded shack. But yet she was a woman, and more handsome than any of the few I have seen in similar circumstance since that day, naked, I mean. She showed no shame at all. She was what she was, human, a woman, subjected to power but not lessened by it, no weaker than before. In the silence that followed I was aware of Lord Hyde's breath coming quick and shallow as the sniggering at the window grew louder.

And then my mama lifted her hands to her hair. Slow and deliberate as before, she unfastened the pins that held the thick auburn tresses in their untidy bun and let them fall about her shoulders and her lovely breasts. It was an insult. She let down her hair for Lord Hyde and so made plain the man's lechery, indeed the lechery of all those who looked at her. The captain had meanwhile dropped to his knees at my mother's feet and was searching through her discarded clothing. Almost at once he discovered a sealed letter in one of her shoes. He placed it on the table.

Lord Hyde broke the seal and shook the letter loose, holding it from him with his gloved fingertips as though it disgusted him. Then he began to read. When the search was over and nothing further discovered, he slipped the letter into his pocket and went out of the room without a word.

It was left to the captain to tell my mother to dress herself.

*　　*　　*

When Lord Hyde returned he brought with him a small glass of cut crystal, a decanter of port wine and also his secretary, a pinched, bitter little Englishman carrying pen, ink and some kind of ledger. The two sat down at the table with the captain and his lordship informed my mama that this hearing was now a court martial and that she was accused of treason. I remember that he examined his fingernails as he spoke these words, and gave the impression that he would rather be hunting foxes than rebels. He poured a glass of wine and tossed it down his throat, then at once poured another one. I was very frightened indeed. Much of what went on I do not remember beyond that my mother treated the court martial with contempt throughout and told them at one point that yes, she was guilty, "if guilt it is to fight you butchers on my own soil."

The secretary scribbled in his ledger. He did not lift his eyes from the table. At another point I remember my mama declaring that she did not recognize the authority of the court for she was a citizen of the United States of America.

—The United States of America do not exist, said the secretary with some distaste. The territories to which you refer, madam, are colonies in a state of rebellion, and it is his lordship's duty to put down that rebellion.

—We ceased to be colonies when we declared our independence.

—What you may or may not have declared is of no matter to us, nor indeed to your rightful sovereign, and that is the king.

My mama fixed her eyes on a point somewhere above his lordship's head. She planted her feet square on the floorboards and presented a figure of defiance. Lord Hyde by now had lost his air of weary lassitude and become visibly irritated by this woman standing before his court martial arguing the legality of the Crown's claims to its colonies. We were then taken out of the room and through the door came the low murmur of the secretary's voice, occasionally interrupted by Lord Hyde or the captain. When we were called back in Lord Hyde wasted no time, and it was with a dull sense of disbelief that I heard him telling my mama that because she had been found guilty of treason he intended to hang her.

—No! screamed Lizzie.

—Be silent! cried the secretary.

I looked up at my mama's face but she

betrayed no sign of emotion whatsoever. She uttered one word only.

—When?

—Tomorrow morning, he said, and then, with a soft laugh—and may God have mercy on your American soul.

I cast my imagination back to that most terrible of days and to the night which followed and I see the last light glimmering red on the hills of Jersey as a figure passes along the ashy road which my mama and Lizzie and I had lately traveled with the soldiers. With the failing light comes the creeping bitter cold of the winter night and in Canvas Town campfires flare and blaze. Dark shapes sit humped close to the flames or move about in shrouded silhouette. There are sudden screams of laughter or pain. To the west the river blinks in the cold light of the rising moon. When he pauses and turns to see what he has left behind him, the lone traveler can make out church spires and the masts of warships moored in the bay and at this hour, with darkness beginning to obscure the devastation done to New York, he can recall the town as it was before the British came.

Some hours later he draws close to the house Lord Hyde has taken for his headquarters. The trees are bare and the land lies hard and fallow, and on a misty morning in January, perhaps, it would make a not unpleasing picture of the earth in repose while it awaits the quickening of life that comes with the spring. But this image of sleep is brutally disturbed by the stark form of a *gibbet* which stands a half-mile beyond the gates of the house. The traveler sees it framed against the sky, alone on its low rise of ground, and the moon shedding a silver light upon that desolate stretch of road. No sight is better calculated to arouse the terror of which he has not yet spoken to a soul, although he has thought of nothing else since being told late that afternoon of what has befallen his mama: that she has been arrested at the Hudson pier then taken to Lord Hyde's house at Kips Bay.

In the moonlight the gibbet throws a long, skinny shadow over the frosty ground and the youth passes across it with downcast eyes. Then he draws close to the house. In several of the windows candlelight glows and in his simple heart he feels a flicker of hope. For where there are men, he thinks, surely there is mercy— foolish boy! Holding fast to this idea he comes to the gates. Two shivering figures huddle close together there.

—Dan!

What Lizzie told him was grim indeed and made more grim still by her anger when she described what had passed between myself and the captain on the pier. She said that I had betrayed our mama and it was all my fault. Never will I forget his anger. It stood between us for the rest of his life, his conviction that if I had kept my wits about me and told a simple lie to the captain all would have been well. He said nothing more but his hot eyes and the rebuke they contained burned into my soul. Dan then approached the sentry at the gate and persuaded him to allow us through. We were permitted to spend what remained of the hours of darkness in an outhouse where once animals had been kept. It stank of manure.

At dawn the house began to stir. Soldiers appeared from various buildings with their tunics open. They shivered and yawned as they crossed the yard to the water barrel. The smell of frying bacon drifted in the clear cold air of the day. From the stables came a shuffling and neighing then the doors were thrown open and a string of horses was led out across the yard, their hooves ringing on the flinty stones and their breath coming like smoke in the chill morning air.

The first of the officers to emerge from the house was the young captain. He approached the outhouse where the three of us were stamping about on the dirt floor trying to get warm. I had slept a little and been awoken by the smell of bacon. It was there in the yard with the soldiers going about their first duties and the horses being led out to the paddock that Dan came face to face with him.

—You have come for your mother, said the captain.

—We have come to beg for her life, said Lizzie.

My sister was a handsome girl and she had our mama's strong spirit. Now she stood pleading softly with the captain.

—If it was in my power, he said, I should spare her, but it is not.

At this we stared aghast at the man. Here was a British officer ready to spare her but pleading impotence! A haughty disdain would have showed better than this tantalizing admission, this glimpse of mercy offered even as it was withdrawn! Lizzie drew close to him.

—Sir, you must help us. If we lose her—

She did not finish the thought. The captain could all too easily picture the circumstances into which the war had thrust us.

—It was the verdict of Lord Hyde himself.

—Then go to him, tell him we shall be in his debt forever, but spare her life!

With this last plea Lizzie gripped the officer's greatcoat and pressed her body against his, gazing into his face with such force of feeling that he had to look away. Still with his face averted he slipped the coat off his shoulders and slung it around the shoulders of the shivering girl before him.

—I will try, he said.

—But let us see her! she cried.

He turned abruptly and walked across the yard to an outhouse not unlike the one in which we had spent the last hours. The door was unlocked and there within we saw our mama. We fell upon her with cries of joy and sorrow mixed.

She was quiet, sad, resigned, but above all concerned for us, her children, and spoke to us not of God's will, nor of the destiny of the republic, nothing of that, but of how we should get by when she was gone. We had less than an hour with her before Lord Hyde appeared and with a nod to the captain indicated that it was time. It was not yet nine in the morning. The captain came to the outhouse door, which now stood open. When my mama saw him an expression of horror touched her features but brief as a breeze on water. Then she stared at him with stony disdain. Lizzie turned to the door.

—No! she cried.

She flew across the room. Setting her fists against the captain's chest she begged for her mother's life.

—I can do nothing more, he said.

—Come, stand by me, said my mama.

With her arms around our shoulders, her throat bare and strands of hair falling loose, my mama stepped into the clear bright morning. Drawn up in the middle of the yard, at attention, with shouldered arms, stood the execution squad, also a boy with a drum. For a moment my mama surveyed the scene as though she was in command of it. Then Lord Hyde stepped forward. He was powdered and painted. We all then followed the execution squad, watched from every window and doorway. Only once did my mama's composure fail her, when the stillness of the morning was broken by the crack of a musket over by the shore. She startled as though the ball had entered her own flesh.

The gibbet stood outlined against a chill blue sky. A noosed rope hung from its crossbeam. Beneath it was drawn up a flatbed wagon with a pair of horses harnessed to it. A squad of redcoats stood to attention in the roadway close by and a small crowd of Americans was gathered a little distance away. The drummer began a slow, muffled roll. A chaplain fell in step beside us and murmured a few words but my mama shook her head and kept her eyes on the road ahead. Lord Hyde moved at a slow, dignified step at the head of the procession and the captain brought up the rear.

When we reached the gibbet the soldiers fell in with the squad already in place there and the rolling drumbeat ceased. The watching Americans were silent. Standing close to the gibbet Lord Hyde slipped off his coat and handed it to the chaplain. In the cold of the morning he stood there, a stout Englishman in a white shirt with lace at the cuffs, an embroidered waistcoat of gold silk and a gleaming white stock with a diamond pin. His wig was powdered as white as his skin, in sharp contrast to his rouged cheeks and scarlet lips.

The captain stepped forward and touched Lizzie on the arm. All at once we realized that we must come away and our mama go forward alone. We embraced her, and the silence was at last broken as from within the crowd of Americans there came a cry of grief which seemed all at once to animate what had become a frozen tableau: the ranked soldiers, Lord Hyde beneath the gibbet, the condemned woman and the watching crowd, and Lizzie now weeping into the chest of the captain while Dan stood by with clenched fists pressed to his bowed head.

Lord Hyde stepped swiftly up on to the wagon and barked at my mama to follow. Only then did it become apparent to all those present that his lordship intended to hang her himself. A murmur of anger was heard and the soldiers stiffened. My mama quickly mounted the wagon, holding her skirts up as she did so. She stood beneath the noose with her head erect and her chin thrust out, her eyes dry and her mouth turned down in an expression of fierce disgust. Her hands were tied behind her back. She refused the blindfold.

She did however wish to speak. The crowd pressed forward. For several minutes all stood in rapt silence. She spoke in a clear voice, her breath turning smoky in the cold of the winter morning, and it was remarkable to me that with Death so close she was unafraid, indeed she seemed at peace, and not because she craved release from a life grown wretched, for she did not. She stood quite still as she spoke and there was no sweeping of the arms, no raising of the clenched fist, for her wrists were tied behind her back. Simply the lifted chin and the shining eyes and the words being *flung out*, so it felt, for nourishment to the Americans present and as poison dashed in the face of the enemy.

—I am not sorry for what I have done! she shouted.

The silence briefly broken by a few ragged cries of assent.

—I am not sorry that I have tried to help my country drive these monsters from our shores!

She gazed out across the wintry scene. We did not move, we made no sound. Her eyes closed for a second. All at once I remembered our house by Trinity Church, and what had become of that place. I believe she was thinking of it too.

—Once, she cried, we lived here in peace, until England became greedy for what was ours! Now I have no wish for peace, I wish for *war*! There must be war if my children are to have peace! My children—

A pause here. With her hands tied behind her back and her head thrust forward she seemed to be pleading with us to acknowledge her sincerity in these the last moments of her life. At last the tears came spilling down her cheeks, and she could not wipe them away. I flung a quick fearful glance at Lizzie, who held her head high, eyes wide and unblinking, her lips parted. I was suddenly afraid the soldiers would seize us, and carry us up onto that wagon, and hang us with our mama. Perhaps she thought the same, for she spoke no more of her children.

—I hate all kings! she shouted. And if by my death—

Now came cries of "Shame!". A rock was hurled from the back of the crowd and struck a redcoat on the shoulder. With a hissed command Lord Hyde held the soldiers in their ranks. It seemed he wanted my mama to empty her heart before he stopped it forever.

—If by my death I help my country then it is not in vain that I am hanged here today!

Then all at once her head sank down and her hair drifted about her face. Hushed silence. No one spoke, no one moved. She seemed to have gone someplace else, somewhere inside herself, perhaps to touch some lodestone of her faith.

Then up came her head again, a fierce light now burning in her damp eyes. Once more she refused contrition, she refused to accept any guilt, refused to admit her wrong. In ringing tones she repeated her former declaration.

—I am not sorry for what I have done!

I later heard it said that her words that day gave inspiration to many in the cause, not least Washington's ragged army. When she was finished there was more cheering and then Lord Hyde placed the noose about her neck. He tightened the knot. He lingered over the task. Still she stood bravely, and still I could not believe that this was the end. Lord Hyde stepped smartly down off the wagon, which shuddered a little. He went forward to take the horses' reins. He nodded at the captain, who drew his sword and lifted it high.

There was nothing in the universe then but a woman standing on a wagon beneath a gibbet, a rope around her neck, her head uplifted in the wind, a faint smile upon her lips—she was looking at *us*, at *me*!—until *down* came the captain's sword—Lord Hyde put the whip to the horses—the wagon lurched forward—

The black vomit will soon begin its awful depredations and when it does my life is measured in hours. The clock ticks on my mantel and the tapping has resumed, but nobody is at the door and I do not trouble to cross the room. I must finish. I have told how I was with her when my mama went to the gibbet and how Lord Hyde conducted the hanging himself—it seems a particular predilection of that noble gentleman to play the hangman. A coffin lay in the back of a wagon and it was in an atmosphere of the bleakest desolation when the crowd had dispersed and the soldiers, all but two, had marched back to the house, that the body of my mama was lifted into it and the lid nailed down. Even now, I can hear their hammers in the stillness of that day! Tap-tap-TAP, tap-tap-TAP!

I stared at the coffin for many minutes. The rough pine box lay so heavy, so *unmoving* beneath the clear sky that it made no sense to think of her there. I had not seen her die. I could not watch when the wagon rolled forward; I had turned my back and closed my eyes and put my fingers in my ears and so I had remained until Lizzie touched my shoulder and said it was over. I stared at the coffin and the sight of it was like an acid in my brain, and it burned so deep that though I forget it in the day, by night I see it again, and again I hear her tapping inside it and know it is beyond me to save her.

I have had a lifetime in which to weigh in the scales of my own conscience the extent of my guilt. It is true that I was only a young boy when I aroused suspicion at the Hudson pier, and my youth goes some way to excusing me. Such is the case for the defense as it might be put before a court of law or a moral tribunal, although the only such body which I recognize, being a godless man, is that which convenes in the dark constricted place to which I have referred before, I mean my soul. And in my own soul's tribunal I am guilty as charged, and deserving of the capital punishment which will soon surely be carried out. And that, you might think, is all there is to it.

It is not. The events of that day and of the day that preceded it left me a haunted man. I suppose it is possible to regard such disorder of the mind as evidence of madness but that would be a mistake. I do not believe I was mad, though I was forced into the kind of existence which the mad know; I mean that my guilt set me apart from others. And it was in that state of wretched solitude that I encountered my mama's ghost, and not once, no, *repeatedly*.

I felt no fear, no horror. Her absence was far more terrible to me than her ghost. It was her absence that did for me! I do not know now how I survived without her and Lizzie was no kind of help or support, being herself broken in spirit after seeing her mama hanged. It was dusk the first time. She stood gazing at the Brooklyn shore where the prison hulk *Jersey* rocked and stank in Wallabout Bay. Somewhere a distant dog was barking. I had seen something from the dock, a human form, a woman standing at the end of the pier, and with a sudden surge of joy I recognized her. Cautiously I advanced along the pier and stood at a little distance from her, careful not to disturb the silence or the twilight or the damp splintered planks beneath my feet. Her hair was lank and her eyes were dead. Her skin had the consistency of lard. She smelled bad. She paid no attention to me but it was enough to be near her. I looked out at the British warships anchored in the bay, their masts thin lines of graphite in the smudged sketch of the evening. They had not burned as Washington had hoped and plotted that they would, I believe because Miles Walsh and my mama and the rest were betrayed. Certainly I never saw Miles Walsh again and can only surmise, from the shrouded fragments which have come down to me in the form of his legend, that he too went to the gibbet, late one night on Barrack Street, or that he died in the Provost or aboard the *Jersey* or any one of the fatal prisons of New York at that time.

I remember that when I returned to Canvas Town and told Lizzie I had seen her she did not properly understand me. She took me to mean that our mama's death had caused me such profound distress that I was unable to thrust her memory from me. But I did not mean that. All that was true but there was something more.

—What more?

She gazed at me with dull eyes red from weeping. Lizzie as I say lost something of her spirit the day my mother was hanged, she ceased to be young. I never again heard her laugh. She never married. And although she lived into the new century she sank into illness during the Madison administration and at the end I believe she was glad to be leaving us, indeed she spoke of joining our parents very soon. She said there was a better place than America and she hoped to reach it. Those were her last words.

—A nightmare, no more than that, she said.

—No, I said. In the light of day.

—Your imagination!

—It does not matter. *I have seen her.*

She said later she would never forget the chill sensation she felt at those words of mine. Many times that summer and fall she came into the town with me. She did not believe me but her need was greater than her doubt. We would go at twilight. I was alert to all movement in the gloom, each footfall in the empty streets, each flickering shape in the glow of a campfire in the places made desolate by war.

—There! Do you see her?

I would seize her sleeve and sink to my knees to stare with trembling, outstretched finger at some shadow, some nothing moving about by the river or down an alley in the quiet parts of the town. She would look where I directed her but saw only rats. Then I would go swiftly forward to pursue whatever it was and she followed me but there was never anything there, not when Lizzie was with me. What was it that I wanted from my dead mama? I do not exaggerate when I say that this question has consumed me down all the wasted years of my life and I believe now that at last I have the answer. I believe that Death, who is very close to me, for we have an appointment a few hours hence—

and is that not Death at my door even now?—
Death whispered the answer to me while I slept
this afternoon. I pursued my dead mama not
because I wanted to *release* her from her coffin,
but because I wanted to be *in* her coffin *with*
her.

There is little left to tell. Half a century has passed
since the Year of the Gibbet, and the war has been
transformed in the minds of my countrymen such
that it now resembles nothing so much as the
glorious enterprise of a small host of heroes and
martyrs sustained by the idea of Liberty and
bound for that reason to prevail in the end.

But I am haunted. I have lived out my days as
a working hack, a lonely little man to be found
with his pipe and bottle in the back parts of the
Rising Sun or some such establishment over by
the East River docks. I have never been free of
my mama. She has shown herself to me on the
shores of Manhattan Island in the hour before
the dawn, it may be, or at dusk, when the light
begins to go. These times, the border times, the
middling uncertain hours when it is neither day
nor night, it was at these times that I would
come upon her as she stood on some abandoned
wharf and I always knew that one day she

would come for me. And this, now, is the time. She is here.

She stands in my doorway with her empty eyes, her soiled clothing open at the seams and her teeth loose in her skull. The noisome odor of the grave is strong upon her. She lifts her pulpy, rotten fingers, and in the street below I hear the death-cart rumble over the cobblestones and come to a halt outside the house. In the back of that death-cart her coffin awaits us and now, at last, as I take my mama's hand, and we move together to the staircase, I know that the contagion is truly upon me.

It is no more than I deserve.

JULIUS

Noah van Horn was a ruddy, raw-boned man with a will of iron, and nobody ever got the better of him in argument except perhaps his daughter Charlotte. To judge from his portrait, which first hung over the mantel in his town-house on Barclay Street, he must have been a quite alarming character in the flesh. Bullish, loud, domineering, impatient—possessed of an ungovernable temper—it is all there in the face, and I say this because the picture is now in my possession and I spend far too much time in front of it. For with his grizzled whiskers and wild black eyes he looks more like an Old Testament prophet than a merchant who spent his days on the South Street wharves—he seems literally about to *burst* from the canvas and lay about the viewer with a stick!

He built the foundations of his fortune in the

63

Atlantic trade, running raw cotton out of Savannah, Georgia, carrying it to London then working his way down the eastern seaboard, turning a profit in every port—this would be the early 1800s and him barely twenty years old. In the decades that followed his wealth rapidly accumulated as he ploughed his profits into shipbuilding, real estate, construction and the like. He may not have been one of the old-money élite, and he was certainly not as devoted as some to the Presbyterian virtues thought conducive to a useful, godly life—sobriety and frugality, to name two—but he had a powerful commitment to aggressive enterprise and the getting of money. In 1832 he married a girl called Ann Griswold who was more than twenty years his junior and the daughter of a Yankee merchant with whom he did business. Over the next years she bore him three daughters, Charlotte being the eldest.

In his domestic life Noah now found some measure of tranquility. He gave up what he thought of as the manly pleasure of drinking brandy with his fellows in the hotels of lower Broadway, and cultivated an interest in the history of ancient civilizations, accumulating a library of some two thousand volumes. In business he continued to prosper, and with him the city. Often he spoke of the day when New York would surpass even London as the greatest port and marketplace in the world, and he said it with the confidence of a man who could expect to pocket a large share of the profits when that day came. But what he did not possess, and for this he would have paid any price at all, was a son.

After the birth of Charlotte, Noah decided to move his young family to a more salubrious location, the business quarter of Manhattan having become increasingly susceptible to the diseases which according to him came in through the port with the Irish and found fertile breeding grounds in the narrow filthy streets and fetid courtyards where they lived. He secured a plot in Waverley Place and set an architect to designing him a house in the Greek manner, all fluted columns, heavy cornices, and triangular pediments—an ugly building which to my eye looked more like a mausoleum than a house. The work was completed in the winter of 1835 and the family moved in. A week later one of the worst disasters ever to befall the city occurred. A fire in a Pearl Street warehouse spread through the downtown business area and in two days destroyed nearly seven hundred buildings, along with tens of millions of dollars-worth of merchandise. Among the private houses burnt to the ground was the recently vacated van Horn residence on Barclay Street. Noah gave thanks. He considered himself blessed.

It was in the house on Waverley Place that Ann van Horn gave birth to the last of her children, and to his great relief Noah finally had a boy. He was christened Julius.

It was a prosperous, established family into which the child was born, but his way would not be easy. When he was an infant his mother died, exhausted by this last delivery; and despite the attention of his sisters, Charlotte in particular, from then on Julius' upbringing lacked the maternal influence which might have tempered his father's unbending severity. For Noah was devastated by the loss of his wife, and in his grief he imposed impossibly high standards on his son. In later life Julius' sisters spoke often of how Noah would beat the little boy for the smallest infractions of the rules of the household. They heard his cries from behind the door of their father's library, and suffered for him, and hated their father. But curiously Julius never seemed to grow bitter at this treatment, for as soon as his tears were dry he would come back as cheerful as before and ask his dear papa if there was anything he might do to be of service to him; and even Noah van Horn, that grim, turbulent man, could not help but be moved by the happy innocence of this gentle child of his.

Noah's intention had always been to educate Julius to take over the House of van Horn when the time came. But he realized before the boy was ten years old that he possessed no sort of a head for business, although what he did possess a head for was not at all clear. In his disappointment he became for a while still more brutal to the child, to the point that Julius emerged weeping from his father's library on one occasion with blood running down his legs, and his daughters could tolerate it no longer. They went in a body, led by Charlotte, and with no little trepidation, to beg their father to desist.

I have often tried to imagine what that interview was like. I know it occurred in the library, a dark, wood-paneled room on the second floor of the house. There were armchairs grouped around a fireplace and a desk made of black mahogany, and bookshelves that rose on every side from floor to ceiling so high that a ladder was required to reach the volumes at the top. The pelt of a bear lay on the floor in front of the fire, the two glass eyes in the massive head staring unblinking into the flames. It was from one of the armchairs beside the fire that Noah barked out the command to enter when Charlotte knocked on the library door that evening.

—Father, we have come to see you on a matter of grave importance to us, she said.

The three girls stood trembling in the light of the gas-lamps as Noah sat with his feet planted wide apart and his hands resting on the arms of his chair, the fingers of one hand lightly curled about the stem of a glass of cut crystal which glittered in the firelight. He wore his smoking jacket, a long, skirted garment of red silk with gleaming dragons emblazoned upon it in gold thread. He wore leather slippers from Morocco. His eyes were hooded, his lip was damp.

—Of grave importance to you.

—To us all, said Hester, modest Hester, by far the mildest of the three. The poor girl was so frightened that no words came when she first spoke, and she had to start again. But like her sisters she gazed with firm resolve into her father's face. Noah crossed his legs at the ankles and set his feet upon the head of the bear.

—I am listening, he said.

Charlotte then took one step forward and still with her hands behind her back she began to tell her father why the beating of Julius must stop. I do not know exactly what was said, but I imagine that as she warmed to her theme her arms grew restive and soon were put to work in service of her argument, and that she became flushed in the face and her voice rose in pitch. Her father, meanwhile, would soon lose the repose he had been enjoying, and the slippered feet came off the head of the bear, the broad brow creased and furrowed—he sprang to his feet and stood over the fire, the color in his cheeks growing ever redder and his hand slapping at his thigh with irritation. The younger girls, emboldened by Charlotte's impassioned plea, were bold enough to cry "Yes!" when their sister grew especially persuasive, and although the entire event took no longer than perhaps ten minutes, by the time Charlotte was finished her father was in a state of some turmoil. He had begun with the simple conviction that Julius required discipline, and plenty of it, and that is what he had believed until Charlotte told him flatly that the boy could not help it that he was what he was.

This idea, strangely, had a profound effect on Noah van Horn, I mean the idea that his son "could not help it that he was what he was." Almost at once, it seems, his feelings toward the boy changed. He saw as though in a blinding revelation that he had been punishing Julius not in order to improve his character but rather to discharge the anger that came with his recognition that the boy would never be as he wished him to be. That he had deceived himself into believing he was preparing Julius for life, when in truth he was indulging his own feelings of frustration and perhaps, too, his widower's grief, which was, as I say, intense—it affected him deeply, and he sank into a state of such despondency that for some days the atmosphere in the house began to affect even Julius' spirits. But at all events, the beatings came to a halt.

The sisters had good cause to feel pleased with themselves. Charlotte was especially gratified that their intervention had proved effective, although in her father's presence she showed nothing of this and for the first and only time in her life behaved as the demure and modest creature she was expected to be, passing through the household and going about her tasks with lowered eyes, and speaking in a voice so quiet as barely to be audible. Her father could not know it, but Charlotte had plans for Julius.

So Noah was forced to abandon his long-held hope that his son would inherit the House of van Horn, and began to look for some young man he could groom as his successor. It was not difficult. New York in those days, as indeed today, did not lack for clever men eager to seize an opportunity to work every hour of the day and night so as to establish their name and their fortune.

It was in many ways an odd choice he made. Where he found Max Rinder I do not know for sure, but although his family came from Bavaria they were not part of that great tide of Europeans which came pouring into New York hot on the heels of the Irish and settled north of the Five Points all the way to Fourteenth Street, so creating a city within the city that had more Germans in it than any other place save Berlin and Vienna!

But that was not Max Rinder. His family had

been on Long Island for two generations, where by all accounts they were contented and industrious, the elder Rinder being something in a brewery. Max, however, had ambition. It may be that he was already a clerk in the van Horn warehouse on Old Slip when he first came to Noah's attention, probably through a display of the kind of qualities Noah would approve—initiative, enterprise, punctuality, deference, or maybe not deference, maybe rather an independence of thought and a readiness to speak up boldly even at the risk of arousing the awful displeasure of the master. He was a sallow young man, above medium height although somewhat stooped, for he had a bony deformity at the top of his spine which is apparent in all the photographs. He had a large sloping brow with a Napoleonic lick of jet-black hair at peak and temple and pale, deep-set eyes—hypnotic eyes, like a snake-charmer or a preacher, which he would fasten unblinking upon whomever he was talking to, the effect unsettling. He was quick in all his movements and even quicker in his thinking, a characteristic particularly esteemed by Noah van Horn, who yielded to no man in his estimate of his own brains when it came to matters of business.

An odd choice, as I say, and it must have saddened Noah to take on this clever young man from Long Island in place of his own son. As for Julius, whom his father had already put to work in his counting-house, no sadness there, none at all—he was delighted at his imminent release from what had become an irksome captivity at a narrow, inky desk and a most tedious set of duties involving the keeping of accounts of bills of lading and cargo manifests and the like. Julius had difficulty with any task involving numbers, indeed with any application of reason to an abstract problem, and this was not his only deficiency, far from it. By all accounts he was a cheerful, friendly boy but he was profoundly disorganized. He was late for his appointments, often lost his money, his house-key, on one occasion his *shoes*, even, and his memory for names was that of an old person suffering from dementia. As to his appearance he was a long-limbed, lanky youth with a chaotic tumble of yellow curls. He grinned wildly when he was pleased or embarrassed and was forever having trouble with his clothing, buttons coming undone, shirt-tails escaping their confinement within his trousers, studs and pins going astray and with them the cuffs and cravats and such which they were intended to secure. His eyesight was poor, and he wore spectacles.

It was Charlotte who saw in him something more than an unkempt buffoon. She watched closely as he amused himself in the sisters' parlor, running off pencil sketches of the girls and their friends and then springing to the piano, where he would invent a tune with a lyric to accompany what he had sketched. Charlotte saw these spontaneous effusions as the froth or spume atop a rising wave of artistic genius, and was determined that her brother not waste it. She was convinced he had the makings of an artist, and it was certainly undeniable that with his wild hair and disheveled aspect he presented the appearance of an artistic *type*, and to artistic *types* the sisters were particularly sensitive.

Without telling anybody what she was doing Charlotte began to look for a teacher for Julius. She visited a dozen studios in New York, most of which housed painters with established reputations. She conducted interviews with each of them. None to her seemed right. She felt that these men were too much like her father in the importance they placed on technique and discipline and industry and the like. Julius would do as he was told, she knew, but there seemed no passion—no "sweet inward burning," as the saying is—until, that is, she met Jerome Brook Franklin. Now here was a man, she felt, for whom art was about more than technique. Here was a man for whom art was life itself.

At that time Jerome Brook Franklin was an impoverished painter of twenty-six whose true calling was the landscape. He had once attended a lecture of Thomas Cole's and come away with the fiery conviction that his life's work lay with the movement to establish a unique American art, an art that did not ape the art of Europe, but assimilated it, rather. *Transcended* it. A new nation, Cole had said—and it was this idea which seared the heart of the young Brook Franklin— required an artistic tradition which reflected its own true spirit, and the true spirit of America lay in the vast sublimities of her boundless unspoiled wilderness. He quoted Emerson: "There I feel that nothing can befall me in life—no disgrace, no calamity (leaving my eyes), which nature cannot repair . . ."

I know very little about art but I have it on good authority that until Thomas Cole arrived, American painters had largely been busy with *ships*, and that it was the merchants who drove the market. At one time Noah van Horn had hanging on his walls a painting of every ship he owned, and this was apparently what art meant to men like him: the precise, impersonal, ostentatious display of one's material property. Handsome enough I suppose if what you like is *rigging*, or the exact color of a *hull*, but hardly the stuff of an emergent civilization. As for Thomas Cole, I remember as a child reading this exchange in a novel. Two men are talking about the wilderness.

—What do you see when you get there? says one.

—Creation! cries the other.

It was to paint pictures of Creation that Jerome Brook Franklin made expeditions into the American wilderness. His canvases displayed sweeping vistas of such scenes of natural beauty as the lakes of northwestern New York in the fall. By that time there was a healthy demand for such paintings, but he had not yet established himself among the more popular artists, and so had to give instruction to young men in order to subsidize his expeditions.

On the day of her appointment Charlotte mounted a narrow flight of stairs to the top floor of a building on West Tenth Street. There was a landing with a banister on one side which overlooked the stairwell all the way down to the lobby. A door stood open and she peered in. What she found was a studio the size of a small ballroom with a bare, uneven wood floor and grimy skylights high overhead. It was empty. The windows were open and from the street below drifted the faint sounds of men, women, horses, and bells. There was a chalky smell in the air with a faint undertone of what she knew to be oil paint. The place was underfurnished. She saw a small stove at the far end, a few rickety tables, a low wooden platform with a number of mismatched cane chairs arranged around it and a wall of shelves holding dusty fragments of the human form in plaster. Elsewhere on the walls were pinned students' sketches of figures in classical poses along with more detailed studies of the human form, and beside a closed door at the back were stacked what she assumed must be the artist's own canvases. Like a throne in the middle of the studio stood a paint-spattered wooden easel with two tall upright arms.

The door at the back swung open and Jerome Brook Franklin emerged. He was burly and full-bearded, with fierce blue eyes, and he wore a checkered suit in a loud pattern of autumnal browns and reds. He advanced upon Charlotte like a bear, took her gloved hand in his own great paw then led her the length of the studio to the back, where they sat close to the stove on a pair of cane chairs. Charlotte said later that he stared at her with a most peculiar intensity, and she experienced some discomfort. She said she liked that. He felt dangerous, she said. To Charlotte this meant he must be a proper artist, and so she told him what she was looking for and what she was prepared to pay. She had brought with her a portfolio of Julius' work, and now she handed it over.

With an air of profound boredom the painter rapidly leafed through Julius' sketches, returned the portfolio, and agreed to take him on. He told her when the new course of classes would be starting, and that seemed to be it. He accepted a part of his fee in advance and stuffed the dollars into the pocket of his vest. Nothing more to be said. Not a man for small talk. Only when she was leaving did it occur to Charlotte to ask him if she might see an example of his own work.

Whatever compunction she might have felt

about making such a request, it was dispelled at once. The painter beamed at her through his whiskers, and without a word went to the canvases propped against the wall. He selected one and hauled it from the stack. It was a big painting, and it required the full stretch of this big man's arms to carry it to the easel. When it was in place he stepped back and the two stood together gazing at it. *In the Catskills at Sunset*, it was called. Charlotte saw a vista of dark peaks receding to the horizon, and beyond them a sky of an intense, pale orangey-blue touched with flames of scarlet radiant against the darker sky over the mountains in the foreground, where in a valley, in utter stillness, lay a lake of what looked like burnished copper and beside it a tiny human figure in a state of rapt contemplation. She stared at it for several minutes. I believe she was genuinely moved. When she turned to the artist her eyes shone with unshed tears.

—It is magnificent, she whispered. You love the place, then?

He nodded.

—I should like to go there once.

He said nothing. She left soon afterwards in a somewhat emotional state. It is hard to imagine that Jerome Brook Franklin was anything but gratified at such a powerful reaction to his work.

It is time, I suppose, that I declare my interest. Jerome Brook Franklin was my grandfather. I met him a few times when I was small, and himself an old man, and in due course will describe an encounter with him—one of the very few glimpses I can provide of any of the actors in this drama at first hand. He was not an easy man but I have reason to believe he was a good man, and he was certainly generous to Julius when he first came out of the insane asylum. I only wish I had known him better.

His studio made as deep an impression on Julius as it had on his sister, and the boy later confessed he was astonished that for so long he should have been unaware that such places existed in the city; and although he could not articulate what it was that excited him so profoundly, he was quite certain that it mattered more than anything he had yet experienced. It was as though a door in his soul, long closed, had been opened, and into the dark place streamed sunlight: this was how Charlotte described her brother's state of mind.

That first morning, he walked up Sixth Avenue to Tenth Street, clutching his portfolio under his arm. He climbed the narrow stairs to the landing at the top, where he found the door was open, so he went in. He was the first to arrive, and for some minutes he wandered about in a state of dawning wonder, just as Charlotte had predicted he would. He then realized that in the room at the far end of the studio a large man in his shirtsleeves and without a collar was bent over a wash-bowl beside an unmade bed. Without turning the man shouted "Early!" and kicked the door shut with a bang. Soon other students arrived, and I can see them all too clearly, those budding young men with their freshness and enthusiasm still intact, each one no doubt privately persuaded of his own unique genius . . . So sad. Not one of them came from a family like Julius', and some I am sure were shabby youths from the tenements who perhaps had to support their studies with ill-paid jobs done at odd hours of the day or night. I imagine they talked about Jerome Brook Franklin, what they had heard about him, what they thought he was like.

He came out at last. It was a brisk morning in early April, and as he walked down the studio he rubbed his hands and cried out to the "young gentlemen" kindly to sit down. He stood on the low platform by the stove and regarded his new students. He then proceeded to talk. Even in old age my grandfather's voice possessed that booming confidence which to impressionable youth carries the unmistakable ring of truth. That day he spoke first of the wilderness, telling them that Nature had the power to "exalt the very bowels of the soul," a phrase that has remained current in my family. He showed them several of his own canvases, and then said that before they could even begin to *think* of painting such pictures they must first study form. They would master the drawing of classical statuary, he said, and then would come the life class. Among the young men there was some grinning and nudging at the thought of the life class, for they had heard stories about artists' models. Only then, said Jerome Brook Franklin—pregnant pause here—only when they had achieved proficiency in the studio would he let them anywhere near a mountain. Julius was in a state of ecstasy by this point.

This was called at the time Julius' "awakening," at least this was what Charlotte called it, who of all the sisters was the most passionate in her conviction of the boy's genius. Not hard to imagine the state he was in when he got back to Waverley Place that afternoon. The three girls were waiting for him of course, and no sooner had they hurried him into the parlor and closed the door than he gazed at them with shining eyes and announced that he was a slave of art for evermore!

Now, to this point Julius' life had been an oddly unstable affair. This was a boy who had lost his mother as an infant and then suffered years of brutality at the hands of a father who to any other child would have quickly become a hateful, terrifying figure, but whom Julius had apparently never feared or hated. Was it possible that he had simply not registered his suffering, just shaken it off? Or that the love of his sisters had in some mysterious fashion *erased* it from his memory? I think not. I believe Julius buried his pain, buried it so deep that nobody saw it, not even himself. Dutifully as a child he had gone to his lessons with his tutors, and later to work in his father's warehouse, and always he did the best he could with such good humor—the wild grin, the flapping shirt-tails, the lost shoes—that despite his manifest limitations no one could find fault with him. But somewhere in the recesses of his heart a mortal wound was weeping.

Charlotte watched him carefully all the while, and as she had anticipated, with this dramatic awakening to art he began to change. He became more aware of the world around him and soon he was never without his sketchbook and pencils. He drew constantly, faces, street scenes, furniture, everything. He made the servants sit for him when they had work to do. He drew his sisters and his father at table, and every afternoon he visited the picture galleries on Broadway. He repeated Jerome Brook Franklin's opinions as though they were his own, and for the first time in his life he gave instructions to a tailor. He ordered several pairs of tight trousers and double-breasted frock coats, and when they arrived he paraded before his sisters like the most absurd peacock. He bought a top hat, a flashy vest, a pair of bright yellow gloves and an eyeglass. It was a marked departure from the republican simplicity of his father's wardrobe—all white stocks and black broadcloth—and it gave particular pleasure to Charlotte, who had accompanied Julius to the shops; in fact Charlotte may well have initiated the whole idea in the first place.

*   *   *

Julius was now ripe for that experience without which no sentimental education is complete, and with the appearance of a girl called Annie Kelly it begins. She was the spark, the match tossed idly into the tinder of Julius' destiny, for with her arrival the fervor so recently aroused in Julius found its outlet. It happened in the studio. There was the usual din of noisy chatter, those boisterous boys waiting to be told what they were to do that day, for no pieces of plaster statuary had been set up for them to work from. They all assumed the room at the back was empty, when suddenly, in the doorway, appeared—a girl. There was an immediate silence. She was clad only in a bed-sheet, which she clutched to her breast. She stood gazing at them as though surprised to find them there. Jerome Brook Franklin at once crossed the studio and led her to the platform.

Annie Kelly was not modest, how could she be, given her line of work? The lack of modesty of artists' models was well known in those days, and gave rise to the popular belief that the morals of such females left much to be desired. Not to put too fine a point on it, they were considered little better than whores, and not a few of them were in fact whores. Annie Kelly was tall and fair, and on the platform, divested of her bed-sheet, she displayed to the astonished youths a pale body perfect in all its proportions. Jerome Brook Franklin arranged her so she stood with one slim hand on her hip and the other at her brow, her face lifted as though to a distant horizon, and one leg bent at the knee: Diana, the huntress. When he was satisfied he turned to the silent, gaping students.

—What is the matter with you all? he cried. Go to work!

It seems they had all been warmly anticipating the coming of the life model, but the reality had taken them very much by surprise. There was some shuffling and coughing, some scraping of chair-legs on floorboards as the shy boys went to their places and prepared to work. Julius sat at his easel staring at the girl. By now he had been working for two months in my grandfather's studio. He had come far, I do not mean as an artist—as an artist he had barely begun—I mean as a sentient being, a creature emerging from the misty innocence of childhood and into mature self-awareness; but for this he was not prepared. Around him his fellows scratched away with their pencils, and after a while he did manage to lift his own, but for a few moments only. Then he set it down again, and looked about him helplessly, suddenly unsure what was happening to him.

I believe that after he left the studio Julius spent the rest of the day on the streets of New York indulging the emotion which had sprung to life in him as he sat gazing at that naked body. At what point he returned home to Waverley Place I do not know, but it seems he had had time enough to decide that what he was experiencing was, in fact, love. When he told Charlotte the extraordinary news, rather than talk carefully to her brother, perhaps advise him to go slow, and be prudent, instead she apparently clapped her hands together, gave out a small scream, cried "Oh, *Julius!*" then flung her arms around him and told him how proud she was.

Then she insisted he tell her everything. In this way Julius' folly was given validity by one who should have know better, for Charlotte was not a child, indeed Charlotte was herself engaged in some related negotiation, though in a spirit altogether different from that of her brother.

* * *

Max Rinder was a man who apparently had "no warmth, no heart, no passion, no nothing." What he did have, it seems, was a swift and devious intelligence and an ability to get what he wanted regardless of what to any other mortal might seem insurmountable obstacles. This utter ruthlessness was a quality he shared with Noah, and it accounted in large measure for the continuing expansion of the House of van Horn. But if he was in some ways like the father, he was as different from the son as he could possibly be, being a wary, cynical sort of a man. Julius by contrast was spontaneous and open, his conversation frequently punctuated by cries of laughter, his body rarely still, and a wide grin overspreading his face as he pushed his fingers through a tumble of unruly curls and adjusted the spectacles forever threatening to fall off his nose.

Over the course of a long New York winter Max Rinder, dressed in his black suit and derby, the collar of his shirt as stiff and starched as the man himself, and those licks of hair as black as bat's wings plastered so close to his skull they might have been painted on it, appeared several times a week at the house on Waverley Place with a judiciously chosen bunch of dried flowers. The object of his attentions was Charlotte van Horn.

Charlotte was now twenty-four and as yet unmarried. She was becoming a cause of some concern to her father. She was not an unattractive girl, as I can attest from a daguerreotype of 1855, but she was difficult. She had frightened off at least two young men who were showing an interest because she was not sufficiently feminine. She was too intense, too loud. Too many opinions. Her father lost sleep over her, for in his gruff way he had a great tenderness for his firstborn child and wanted to see her safely settled in the world.

None of which escaped Max Rinder. He had seen from the very outset that a man of property like Noah van Horn, with his three unmarried daughters, could provide the means of fulfilment of all his ambitions. He recognized Charlotte's predicament, and he also recognized the depths of her father's feelings for her even if no one else did, including Charlotte herself. He began to woo her. Not hard to conceive what a very odd wooing it was, not least because despite being at first rebuffed with some hilarity, he continued earnestly to insist upon the sincerity of his intentions until slowly his presence in the house became accepted. In his pinched way he actually seemed to enjoy Charlotte's extravagant talk, her smoking of cigarettes and her dangerous ideas. Charlotte was an abolitionist, and she believed in free love.

Noah van Horn watched the courtship with quiet amusement and also with keen interest. He knew Max Rinder's worth, and if, as I suspect, at root he thoroughly disliked him, that had no bearing on the younger man's genius in the field of business. So the idea of binding him closer to the House of van Horn by bringing him into the family was one of which Noah shrewdly approved. From his point of view, at one stroke the futures both of his daughter and of the firm would be secured. So his partner's visits to Waverley Place were discreetly encouraged, with the result that after some weeks the younger sisters abandoned the parlor to the couple. They would press their ears to the door but they heard nothing, and what went on in there remained a mystery. The very idea of Rinder expressing the contents of a brimming heart was enough to send them all into fits of laughter.

As for Charlotte, she told her sisters that once they got to know Rinder—she always referred to him by his surname, as though such a man could have no other, and pronounced it RYN-der—they would come to like him as much as she did. She allowed that there was at times a certain *chill* in his manner, but assured them it would disappear when he grew more familiar with the family, and it with him. In fact what Charlotte had to her surprise discovered in this complicated young man was, I believe, of all things—vulnerability. An intense sensitivity to pain which he concealed from everybody except her. For he had suffered much in his dramatic rise in the world of trade and commerce, and he was not thick-skinned. Every insult, every slight drew blood and caused deep hurt, and he was unable to forget such wounds. He schemed and brooded, and did not see that this was a sickness.

But Charlotte did. Charlotte was moved by Rinder's pride and his private suffering, and she pitied him. She offered him sympathy, and tried to deflect him from his fantasies of revenge. Rinder was not a stupid man and he responded at once to Charlotte's overtures, for he had never known intimacy before and had no notion of the power of a woman's comfort, his own mother having provided him none. In this he was oddly like Julius, and I believe it is probable that Charlotte recognized in Rinder the same deep need she saw in her brother, so that in a way Rinder now became the boy's rival, in fact his replacement. Julius did not realize this. He felt only joy that his sister should be finding happiness in love, and he welcomed his rival into the house with unfeigned warmth.

The couple was married in the early spring of 1857. Noah escorted his daughter into the First Presbyterian Church on Fifth Avenue, Charlotte in a white satin dress with a long train and a tulle veil which fell like a mist from a headpiece of daisies and lilies. She was transformed from the Charlotte they all knew, the restless, excitable young woman so quick to argument, so intemperate in her enthusiasms. Instead she seemed demure, at peace—in love, even. Rinder himself achieved a kind of brooding glamour, for no one had ever glimpsed in him anything remotely approaching happiness before and it rendered him almost handsome, in a saturnine sort of a way. Charlotte's sisters were her bridesmaids and the best man was a brother of Rinder's from Long Island; there is a daguerreotype of this group too.

Back at Waverley Place the happy couple attended a reception with family and friends before leaving for a short honeymoon in Florida. As the carriage drove away one of the guests was heard to say that "poor Charlotte doesn't realize that her doll is stuffed with sawdust." I personally think Charlotte was quite well aware that her doll was stuffed with sawdust, but she also knew that that was not all he was stuffed with. The point, though, was that he was *her* doll, and as far as that went neither Hester nor her younger sister Sarah had a doll to call her own, sawdust-filled or otherwise.

By the time they had returned and settled into a house in the West Twenties life in Waverley Place had changed forever. Without Charlotte the house lacked a certain feverishness. Charlotte had made the sisters' parlor a place where gossip and laughter and lively conversation about subjects artistic and political were encouraged, but in her absence the house became almost somber. The girls read more, chattered less, and plied their needles as they never had before. Julius barely noticed. In fact Julius, obsessed as he was with Annie Kelly, contributed significantly to the subdued atmosphere, and without Charlotte he wandered about, a lovesick youth, absorbed in the eruption of a volcanic passion but with nobody to talk to about it.

But what exactly had passed between him and the girl? It seems that without Charlotte to confide in, Julius became secretive, and later no one could be sure how much contact he had actually had with her. But the next time the girl worked in the West Tenth studio I feel sure that this lanky, grinning art student actually attempted to shake her hand as she took her place on the platform. To general amusement Jerome Brook Franklin at once came stamping across the floor, clapping his hands and crying out that that was enough, there was to be no nonsense, they were here to *work*!

When the class was over and the other students had dispersed he waited for her outside the building. Her hair was pinned up now in a large heap at the back of her neck, and she wore a straw bonnet with a broad brim. About her shoulders was thrown a lace shawl and her skirt was unencumbered by hoops or petticoats or any of the other clutter that respectable girls wore in those days. She was shod in scuffed black boots with buttons up the side and on her arm she carried a basket. She was a tall, jaunty, handsome girl and Julius fell in beside her as she strode east on Tenth Street. She affected to ignore him but he was so persistent that she at last relented and told him her name.

She then climbed aboard a horse-car going south on Broadway. But having seated herself she saw that he was hanging on the platform at the back of the carriage and she rolled her eyes to heaven, for she was no stranger to importunate youths like this. Then he was pushing through the standing passengers with copious apologies until he stood in front of her, clinging to the pole and grinning at her. She knew he was a rich boy and she was wary of him, but all the same he did amuse her a little. With every lurch of the carriage he was flung this way and that, but still he hung over her, and she consented to talk to him.

I see them descend from the horse-car somewhere in the vicinity of City Hall, where she sat with him on a bench in the park. She told him a little about herself, that her mother had a boarding-house on Nassau Street, and then they spoke about Jerome Brook Franklin. After a few minutes the bells of St. Paul's reminded the girl that she had duties at home, and away she went. She paused at the gate of the park. Julius stood by the bench with his hand outstretched and a blissful smile on his foolish face.

Then see the love-struck youth make his slow way back up Broadway! He had, yes, properly fallen in love. He had not however fallen in love wisely, but why should he? Who falls in love wisely? He could not guess that the thing would end in tragedy. I almost think his feet were a few inches above the sidewalk, and as the crowds swept by him he barely heard the tumult of voices, the wagons and carriages, the fruit-sellers and cigar-sellers and the newsboys with their penny papers crying out the latest murder—none of it touched Julius. He walked home in a kind of sanctified silence.

In those days—this would be the summer of 1859—all over New York buildings were going up, others coming down, some no more than ten years old, but in this impatient town where nothing ever has a chance to decay, ten years was practically an eternity. Up beyond Harlem Heights surveyed lots which were no more than granite outcrops with perhaps a few trees, some stagnant swampland, here and there a squatter's shack and a dirt road running through it would soon be leveled, the swamps drained, the site turned into prime building land in a city whose expansion was limited only by its riverbanks.

"Man marks the earth with ruin; his control
Stops with the shore."

Or so thought the poet Byron. None of which
however had any immediate relevance to Julius
van Horn. For him the din and chaos of a city
engaged in an unending turmoil of construction
was nothing more than a spectacle provided for
his amusement. It was theater, and this being a
period when increasing numbers of Europeans
were arriving in Manhattan every day, the
streets became more diverse, more colorful
and exotic with every ship that discharged its
cargo of humanity at the Battery. Julius liked
the strange accents, the incomprehensible lan-
guages he heard spoken on the streets, and when
she let him accompany her downtown he imi-
tated these alien voices to Annie Kelly, who
herself being only two generations away from
the old country—Ireland, of course—shouted
with laughter at his mimicry. And if more
somber tones were sounding in the air about
them, if the newspapers grew daily more dire in
their predictions of open conflict between the
northern states and the South, none of that
touched Julius, for he had no time for newspapers and politics.

The same was not true of his father. The long-simmering dispute over slavery went to the very heart of Noah's cotton interests, for he held bonds from southern planters worth tens of thousands of dollars; like many New York merchants he was apprehensive as to what would happen next. He was not so apprehensive, however, that he failed to take note of his son's changed mood. One night at dinner he suddenly asked Julius what was the matter with him, and the boy was surprised to feel a sharp kick on the shin. His sisters had warned him to say nothing about Annie Kelly.

—Nothing, father, he said, and gazed at his stern papa with bright eyes in which it was not hard to discern the fear of one who has all his life been innocent of any attempt at deception, particularly in his own home, but who for the first time has *lied*, if only by omission.

Noah frowned at his plate then cut his meat with some deliberation. The silence deepened about him and Hester attempted to change the subject.

—They say it will rain tomorrow, she began, but her father without a sound, without lifting his head, set down his knife and raised his hand slightly, and Hester fell silent. Once more clouds of unease and discomfort began to gather in the room. I have heard about the terrifying power of Noah's silence, when he chose to exercise it— so terrifying that its reputation came down through the family as though it were a legend, or an anecdote, at least, of some historic import, such as might be told if a great man had come to dinner at the house: Daniel Webster, for example, with whom Noah was acquainted. Such at any rate was the repute of his silences, and it seems he deployed one now.

Poor Julius was ill-equipped for the immense reserves of—what?—skepticism, disapproval, disdain, even, that charged the atmosphere when his father perpetrated a silence. He began to fidget. He squirmed. He dropped his fork, and the clangor of cutlery on bone china was very dreadful in the stillness of the dining room. At last Noah lay down his knife and fork, set them side by side across his plate, and lifted his head.

Oh, it was a noble head! A large head, and in the man's maturity—Noah was over seventy now—his whiskers were clipped and gray, a salt-and-pepper beard which by means of its concealment of his cheeks and jaw drew one's gaze to the wise black eyes and the broad forehead on which a few last strands of silver were brushed straight back. The eyes came to rest with a gathering intensity upon the distressed figure of his son. At last he spoke.

—What is it you are not telling me, son?

—Nothing, papa!

Another few seconds of that frightful gaze upon him, and poor Julius wished only to be lifted bodily by a team of angels and spirited off to some remote place. Then Noah pushed back his chair, rose to his feet and, plucking the starched white napkin from his throat, flung it onto the table. Still regarding Julius, with an expression now of hurt, as though the boy had insulted him, he left the room.

No sooner had the door closed than Julius burst into tears and laid his head on his arms on the table. His sisters rushed to him and with their arms about his heaving shoulders begged him not to cry, it was all right, everything was all right—

—It's not all right! cried Julius, lifting his head and turning to them, and as he did so the last of the evening sunlight fell full upon him, and his cheeks shone with tears, his hair gleamed like gold.

—It's not all right, he said more quietly, but with a desperate throb of sorrow in his voice. I have told papa a lie!

—Not a lie, said Hester, stroking his head.

—I must tell him about her, he whispered, his damp eyes fierce now.

—Not yet, I beg you, dear brother.

I think this may have been the first time Julius properly understood the necessity of behaving in the world with less than utter transparency. Never before had he had to conceal his feelings, though I remind myself of what he must surely have concealed as a small boy, when his papa had beaten him until he bled.

Noah meanwhile sat in his library upstairs and pondered what had just occurred. There are versions of Julius' story in which Noah assumes the appearance of a one-dimensional figure whose sole function it was to punish and constrict, but I am not so sure. I believe he had come to regard with deep remorse the man he had once been, and recognized that his own grief and loneliness after the death of his wife were responsible for the rage which was discharged at Julius; or even, in his blindness, that he had *blamed* Julius for the death of his wife. And the fact that the boy had grown up with no apparent residue of bitterness disturbed him now, for he was too honest with himself to believe that his violence had had no consequence.

All this I imagine going on behind the grimly frowning façade of the bearded man who padded about the large house on Waverley Place during the fraught summer of 1859. Nor could he take any comfort from his daughters. He knew them to be entirely partial to Julius, and none of them wise enough quietly to seek their father's counsel save, perhaps, Charlotte. But Charlotte lived now with her husband, with Rinder, and was only rarely in the house on Waverley Place. So Noah decided that he would try to find common ground with his son without Charlotte's mediation, and break down the barrier of silence which had arisen between them. After dinner one evening he asked Julius to walk with him in Washington Square while he smoked a cigar.

This was a pleasure Noah had for many years indulged during the summer months, although perhaps *pleasure* is not the right word. For those strolls around Washington Square had once been taken in the company of his wife, and very delightful it must have been, I am sure, for this driven man to speak quietly of his day and be assured of an intelligent feminine sympathy. But since Ann's death the evening stroll had become a thing of sorrow and nostalgia, and beneath those ancient sycamores he often allowed his grief to rise to the surface, and the occasional fugitive tear to fall—"nor did all the Pacific contain such wealth as that one wee drop," as Herman Melville had written a few years earlier about another troubled American. When Noah returned to the house and put his key in the front door, he was not at peace, as once he had been, but was, rather, almost overwhelmed at the loss of the woman who had once brought meaning to all he did.

So one evening he took Julius with him. The boy was nervous, of course. For almost two weeks he had been trying to conceal from his father the fact that he was in love, and the strain was acute. He longed to burst forth with all he felt, pour it out and lay it before him, have his father nod and grunt and then perhaps say something wise, as had so often happened in his childhood after the dreadful early years. How important his papa's sympathy had been to Julius! And now he had deprived himself of it. How he longed to make things right and clear between them once more, but had not his sisters warned him that his father would forbid him to see Annie Kelly, should he come to hear of their friendship?

It was a sultry evening early in July. They left the house together and were watched from the parlor window by Hester and Sarah, who of course understood the implications of this walk in Washington Square. Noah paused on the sidewalk as was his habit, and took some moments to light his cigar. He considered talking to Julius about Havana, where he had just opened an office. But on reflection he decided that silence would more quickly loose the stream of the boy's mind.

And so they walked in silence, and as his father expected, Julius soon became agitated, and then could hold back no longer.

—Father.

Noah inclined his head. The heat of the day had passed off a couple of hours before, and the warmth of the evening was pleasant, the air thick with the fragrance of foliage and flowers, and as they followed the path around the square they bowed to other well-to-do New Yorkers who had come out of houses not unlike their own to enjoy the evening.

—Father, is it ever wrong to love?

Familiar though he was with the naivety of his son, Noah could not restrain a bark of laughter.

—Is it wrong? How could it be wrong to love? he said.

Then all at once Noah understood that he had given away the first point in the game by admitting the absolute value of love. Poor Julius, he did not even know he was playing a game, nor that he had seized the advantage effortlessly by failing to employ a stratagem. He agreed with some alacrity that no, of course it could not be wrong to love, how could it be? And more in this vein. When his outburst was over his father allowed a few seconds of silence and then spoke again.

—And who is it you love, son? You love your sisters, I know. I may hope you love your father.

Now this was a stratagem. Julius at once plunged into the trap.

—Of course I do, papa, but this is not the same.

—What is not the same?

There. They were at the crux of the thing already.

—Why, it is different!

—That is surely what we mean by "not the same," said Noah, dryly.

Julius made an inarticulate sound. He was encouraged. He could hold it back no longer.

—I love a girl, papa!

—Ah. That is different.

—It is different, papa!

—To love a girl is certainly different from loving your sisters.

—It is not the same at all, papa!

—I think we have established it. Who is she?

This was the moment, the boy knew, about which his sisters had warned him.

—You will be angry with me.

—But why?

—Her name is Annie Kelly.

Here was the first realization on Noah van Horn's part that Julius had not chosen a girl of his own class. He knew no Kellys. He did not doubt, however, that the human cargo of the Atlantic packets, discharged daily at the southern tip of the island, contained many a Kelly.

—And what do her people do, son?

—Her mother keeps a boarding-house on Nassau Street.

Another silence, as father and son turned at the end of the square. The father walked slowly with his hands behind his back, his head lowered, the cigar between his teeth. Julius, beside him, seemed all arms and legs, his face alive with shifting emotions, now biting his lip in acute agitation, now grinning at the branches over-head. He twisted like a fish on a line which leaps from the water when the line is jerked.

—I should like to meet her. Will you bring her to the house?

Would he? For this his sisters had not pre-pared him. He was alarmed but did not know why. He had no guile and he could think of no reason to refuse his father. But all the same it was, I am sure, with some anxiety, some fore-boding, even, that he agreed to bring Annie Kelly to the house. They walked home in silence. When they reached the front door Noah turned to his son. He saw how impressionable the boy was, how innocent. How *gullible*. He was aware of a distinct surge of anger, its object the Kelly women. He grew cold. He would crush them if he had to. But he showed Julius nothing of this. He opened the front door and ushered his son into the warm gloom of the hall. Julius' sisters appeared in the parlor doorway.

—Here he is, said Noah. You may have him back now.

It had become Julius' habit after the life class to wait for Annie under an awning on the south side of Tenth Street, and sometimes they would wander downtown together, or perhaps take a horse-car, pausing in City Hall Park to sit by the Croton Fountain before Annie went to her chores in the boarding-house. I believe Annie had no delusions about her feelings for Julius. He was far less worldly than she was but he amused her, this laughing boy, and with him she could shed her tough skin. He was like a brother, and she was, I think, genuinely fond of him. One day shortly after his conversation with his father she saw him waiting for her as usual and ran across the street to him, heedless of the cry of a cartman high on a wagon piled with barrels. She pushed back the brim of his hat and pulled loose his cravat. Their affection for each other was largely expressed in pullings and pushings, little kicks and slaps and such. Julius being a transparent youth, that day his mood was evident in the pull of his mouth, the sag of his shoulders, his whole sorry aspect.

—What is it? cried Annie. You are ill!

He shook his head, and as they set off along the street she turned toward him, concerned to discover what ailed her friend.

—What did he say to you? she said.

He did not have to ask her who she meant. "He" was always Jerome Brook Franklin.

—He did not say anything to me, said Julius.

—What then? Tell me!

She was fierce and urgent, clutching his arm as he shambled along the street, people surging past them, all in far too much of a hurry to take in the spectacle of this tall disheveled youth and the lovely girl hanging onto his arm and peering into his face, demanding that he tell her what was wrong.

—Tell me, Julius, or I shall cry!

The effect was immediate. Oh, but to make her *cry*—! Julius was horrified. He stopped dead and stared at her. The crowds streaming along the sidewalk now began to take notice of them, for they had become an obstacle and had to be steered round.

—No, don't cry!

—Then tell me.

So he told her that his father wanted him to bring her to the house.

—To the house?

She thought about this a moment.

—Well, why not? she said.

Bold girl, she did not think the prospect so bad. She *wanted* to meet his father, she said, and his sisters too. Why should she not? What had she to fear? Julius said he did not know.

—Then why so blue?

Then he told her that Charlotte had said that their father would try to break up their friendship. Annie was indignant. Why would he want to do that? she said, though I think she knew the answer. They walked on in silence and turned down Broadway. They became aware of the roar of the great thoroughfare.

—I don't know, said Julius at last.

—Then stop it. It will be alright. Never mind what Charlotte says.

This was new. It had not occurred to Julius to never mind what Charlotte said, and the idea that Annie might possess an authority equal to his sister's came upon him with some force. Always he had deferred to Charlotte, assuming in her a wisdom he would never possess. To think that Annie Kelly also partook of that mysterious female knowledge, and that he could turn to her now—to Julius this had the impact of divine revelation. In that instant he abandoned all dread at the prospect of her coming to the house. He remembered his father's affection, and knew that papa would see what he, Julius, saw in her. Charlotte was wrong! He said this to Annie, but now the girl would say not a word against this sister she had not yet met.

I have given some thought to Annie Kelly's reaction to this proposed meeting with Julius' father. There are those who believe that the girl was motivated simply by avarice, and recognized in the invitation an opportunity to move closer to what really interested her, that is, the van Horn money. But I do not think she was so mercenary as that. I believe she was simply curious, and thought she had nothing to lose. She may have wondered idly whether something to her advantage would come of it, but I do not think she had any sort of a plan. It would be wrong to be too cynical about the girl.

The sisters greeted her at the front door. It seems they took a liking to each other at once, and if Annie had started to feel at all apprehensive about the evening, her worries were quickly put to rest. The three girls hurried her into their parlor and made her welcome. They hung up her bonnet and admired her dress, a homemade garment of green velvet. Charlotte sat with her on the little sofa by the window, and as Annie looked about her, impressed by all the books and paintings, and the open piano with pages of music loosely stacked on top, she gave her a cigarette.

—You smoke, of course, she said.

—Charlotte says we must all smoke, cried Sarah, but you don't have to!

Worldly though she was, Annie had never smoked a cigarette, but it seemed a good time to start. Hester and Sarah clapped with delight as she took her first puff and of course spluttered and coughed and turned red in the face.

—It isn't easy, said Charlotte. You must practise.

—It's horrid! shouted Hester. You see, Charlotte, she hates it!

—I don't hate it, said Annie, recovering, but I have not the gift.

But she tried again, with more success.

—Charlotte told Julius he may not join us, said Sarah, because we wanted to have you to ourselves. Do you mind?

—I do not, said Annie. It's nice, us all girls together. Is it your own room?

—We sometimes allow Julius in here, said Charlotte, if we want to be entertained.

—Well, he's a grand entertainer, said Annie— and so it went on. Soon they were asking her the question uppermost in their minds, which was how she could go in front of men without any clothes on, and she told them she was sure that

God didn't object, for hadn't He made her body in the first place?

—But you mustn't tell father, said Hester, because he wouldn't understand.

—What am I to say then? said Annie.

—Say nothing, said Charlotte, and I will do the talking.

A little later there came a knock at the door.

—Go away, Julius, they shouted, and hooted with laughter. But he came in anyway, wreathed in large grins because his sisters approved of his friend. By the time they heard the dinner gong they were all quite delighted with one another.

They passed into the hall. Coming down the stairs from his library was Noah, dressed for dinner, and behind him came Rinder. Both men paused, and Annie gazed up at them. The hilarity which had followed them out of the parlor dissipated. Noah was grave. Not for a moment did he betray his feelings. He already disapproved of her, in a sense he feared her. It was impossible for him to think of a girl called Kelly without the taint of her race upon her, and in the New York of those days that taint be-spoke lives of squalor and drunkenness in the crowded tenements of the Points and the Hook. This was the burden of prejudice with which

Noah regarded his son's friend from the staircase of his home that evening, and her slim,
straight figure and flawless skin served only to
sharpen his suspicion, for now he understood
that the threat she posed was greater than he
had first imagined.

He continued down the staircase and gave the
girl his hand. Annie showed proper respect, the
father's stiff formality being exactly what she
expected of a man of his station, and as the
sisters filled the air with chatter so as to steer
them through the first fraught phase of the
encounter she took Noah's proffered arm and
together they walked into the dining room.
Julius grinned at the ceiling and bit his lip,
and as for Rinder, he had given little thought
to this Irish girl whom Charlotte was so eager to
meet. But all that changed when he saw the girl.
For he was at once strongly attracted to her, and
for the rest of the evening kept a furtive eye on
her.

Noah showed nothing of his feelings. He was
surprised to discover that the girl was not frightened of him, and found himself after a while
feeling almost affectionate toward her. In other
circumstances he might have made much of her,
for she lacked what he regarded as the peculiar

foolishness of his own sheltered daughters. At one point he scanned the table and realized that other than himself and Rinder she was the only real adult present, for even Charlotte knew little more than theaters and picture galleries and drawing rooms. But he knew that her confidence came of a greater level of contact with men, and this disturbed him. He did not know that the girl modeled for artists but he sensed her lack of proper feminine modesty. No, she would not do, not for his son, and it was with some distaste that he recognized how unpleasant it was going to be to break the thing up. He did not want to hurt Julius but it could not go on, this he had known since the boy told him in Washington Square who she was. His touch would have to be sure and subtle, and he was irritated by the prospect.

None of which was apparent to his children. Was it apparent to Annie? I think not. I do not believe she had encountered a man like Noah van Horn before. She did not know how such men felt with regard to the assimilation into their established world of the immigrant masses. Noah employed Irishmen on his wharves, his ships, his building sites and in his warehouses, and while he knew many who were sober and industrious men, nonetheless he believed them at root to be a shiftless, dishonest people. He would employ them, but allow one of their women to draw close to his children, to befriend his daughters and walk out with his son—it must be stopped, and the sooner the better. None of this, as I say, was apparent to the young people who sat at his table that night, and when dinner ended and Noah retired once more to his library with Rinder, they decided with joy and relief that the thing had gone off splendidly.

Noah was nothing if not decisive, but for once in his life he found himself reluctant to do what he knew he must. He spoke of the matter to his son-in-law that very night. He told Rinder what was on his mind.

—She won't do, he said.

Rinder himself came of immigrant stock. He had clawed his way into society, had become a partner in the House of van Horn, had married into the family—all good reasons why others must be prevented from doing the same. He must thwart this upstart girl, despite the fact that she aroused him—or *because* she did, perhaps—or the family would begin to look like a way-station for every aspiring nobody in New

York. He was astonished that his father-in-law could have allowed the thing to progress this far, but he understood the reason.

—Why not leave it to me? he said.

It went no further that night. Charlotte appeared in the library some moments later to ask Rinder please to take her home. I next see the two men in Noah's office in the warehouse on Old Slip. I see Noah at the window, frowning, his hands thrust deep in his pockets. I see him turning toward the younger man.

—Leave it to you?

He regarded his partner with some suspicion. In all the years they had known each other Noah had often been surprised by Rinder. A generation younger than Noah, Rinder regarded the city as a lawless territory where ferocity, speed and cunning counted most: a state of nature. More than once he had made the argument to Noah that they served the market, and what the market demanded they must supply, for if they did not then the next man would and he would prosper and they would fail.

Noah disliked thinking of himself as a servant of the market, as a servant of anything, in fact, but he recognized an ugly truth in what Rinder believed, even if he no longer acknowledged the brutal rapacity of his own activities as a young man. But why should Rinder take care of the Annie Kelly problem?

—I know girls like that, he said.

He had identified precisely what troubled Julius' father: "girls like that" were girls who preyed on gullible young men. Rinder was closer than Noah to the street, where such girls flourished. Noah saw the point. He assumed there would be a payment made.

—Not overly generous, he said.

—Of course not.

—And Julius must know nothing.

He held the other man's eye. A profound importance attached to Julius remaining ignorant of the scheme.

—He must think she has tired of him.

—He will know nothing of it.

—You relieve me of a tiresome burden.

Rinder bowed slightly. So stiff was he, this thin, ageless creature in his black clothes you might almost expect to hear a creaking sound when he bowed from the waist. Rinder's ambition, his sole ambition, was to assume control of all that Noah van Horn possessed. It had been his habit in recent years to take on whatever Noah found distasteful, and the problem of Annie Kelly was distasteful in the extreme.

Rinder left the room and Noah settled at his desk with a sense of relief which was not altogether comfortable. He was still troubled. It was an instance of an almost imperceptible slackening in his control of his own affairs that he should so quickly have allowed his partner to assume responsibility in this matter. Noah was at last growing tired. For more than forty years he had run the House of van Horn and overseen its steady expansion. He was now among the wealthiest men in New York. He believed that in a few more years he would retire. To travel, perhaps, and to read. He had for years wished that he had more time to spend in his library. He wanted to study the ancient civilizations, for he was curious to draw comparisons between those civilizations and his own. He believed that the American people would in time be as great as any in human history, and he wanted to spend a year in Europe to visit the old sites, the ruins. He would take Julius with him, perhaps set him up with a teacher in Paris, or in one of the German studios. Alone each evening in his library, Noah thought often of this happy prospect, and Rinder, he was confident, would make it possible by assuming the responsibilities he was finding increasingly irksome.

So Noah permitted himself a sigh of relief. Five more years, he thought, possibly four. Julius would then be twenty-two. He would take the boy to Europe and they would see together what the Old World had to offer the New. He had recently read that the coming of the great cosmopolitan city marked the beginning of the last phase of a civilization, the city being a sure symptom of imminent degeneration and decay. As he sat there in his office on Old Slip, he lifted his head from the papers before him and regarded the wharves and piers built out into the East River to north and south as far as the eye could see, and from the vessels crowded at those wharves a forest of masts rising high as church spires in the shimmering air of the morning. More shipping lay at anchor out in the river and the Upper Bay beyond, among them his own clipper ships, narrow, high-masted vessels which crossed the Atlantic faster even than the steam-driven packets; and seeing all this he knew that what lay ahead was not the first stage of decay but the last preparation for greatness, or more than greatness, for

New York's triumphant assumption, rather, of the mantle of distinction of being not only the pre-eminent city of America, but of the world.

He then reflected that he must be getting old. He had never had time to think thoughts of such foolish grandiosity when he was a young man. With a snort of amusement he went back to work.

A week later Julius appeared in the studio and discovered that there was no model for the life class. The students were working from pieces of plaster statuary. He approached Jerome Brook Franklin.

—Where is she, sir? he said.

The painter was attempting to open a window that was stuck. The day was a hot one, and he was warmly perspiring.

—How should I know? he said, between grunts. She was meant to come to me yesterday. I waited an hour. Damn!

The window continued to refuse to move.

—She was meant to come to you? said Julius.

Brook Franklin turned to him with considerable ill humor.

—I waited an hour! Waste of time! She's gone to hell for all I care.

This was the first Julius knew of Annie's private modeling sessions with Brook Franklin. It did nothing to allay his sense of unease, rather it increased it. But had no one gone to Nassau Street to see if she was at home? No one had.

An hour later Julius walked east to Broadway and boarded a horse-car going downtown. He got off at Warren Street and crossed the park where they had so often sat together, and made his way down Beekman to Nassau. Then he was hammering at the door of the boarding-house, and a few seconds passed before it was opened by Mrs. Kelly. At once Julius knew there was no good news.

—Have you seen her? she cried. Is she with you?

She stepped past him and scanned the side-walk beyond, as though he might be trailing the girl behind him. Julius had been inside the house on several occasions, and had come to know Annie's mother. She was a plump, jovial woman with skin as clear and youthful as her daughter's. She had lived all her life on the east side of lower Manhattan, having been an actress once and played in all the local theaters. She later married a ship's carpenter, raised several children and saw enough riotous times not to be

shocked by anything now. In her narrow hallway, on a threadbare carpet with the smell of
boiling vegetables seeping from the back parts
of the house, she told Julius what had happened,
or rather what had not happened. Three days
before, a Sunday, Annie had left the house early
in the morning, saying she would not be home
until dinner-time. She had not said where she
was going. She had not been seen since.

—Where could she be? cried Julius.

—Oh dear God if only I knew! cried Mrs.
Kelly. And her with only the clothes on her
back!

She began to weep, and Julius took her in his
arms. They clung shuddering to each other for a
few seconds. Julius stepped back. He clutched
her shoulders, and the one tear-streaked face
stared into the other. He asked her what had
been done, and she told him that the men in the
house had been out looking for her every night,
and had told the police, and all the neighbors
knew she was missing, but nobody had seen her.

—I had thought she was coming to you! she
cried.

This brought on further sobbing, and it was
another half-hour before Julius could leave the
house. He sat on a bench in the park and tried to

think what to do. How could she allow her mother and now himself to suffer such anxiety? Was she dead? Then he was running down to the East River to find his father, but Noah was not there. Julius was frightened now. He could not shake off the feeling that Jerome Brook Franklin was involved, for this news of the private sessions unsettled him. He ran through the seaport scanning the crowds for a glimpse of her, groping in his mind for an answer. Dead or captive, he thought. The docks were crowded with wagons and barrows, with men, with ships, crates and bales, stacked barrels, officials of the Port of New York with their papers and pens and watch-fobs, a storm of talk and shouting and drifting through it this distraught youth staring hard at any young woman who passed him, his lips trembling as he murmured to himself, although nobody could have made out what he was saying even if they had the inclination to, which they didn't. Gulls screamed and horseshoes clanged on cobblestones, there was salt in the wind and great pungent drafts of beery odor issued from the South Street taverns. Pennants flapped from yards and masts and bare-chested Irishmen rose up from cargo holds like heroes from the underworld, while in the upper stories of warehouses shouting clerks winched up barrels by means of hoisting wheels, and merchants with aprons round their waists and cigars between their teeth added their own voices to the din. But in all this hectic humanity no sign of Annie Kelly.

He reached Bowling Green and there at the very foot of Broadway he turned north. It was as good a place as any to search for her, and besides, a simple plan had begun to take shape amid the wild lunges of his disordered mind. He would go back to Tenth Street and talk to Brook Franklin, ask the man's help. Discover why she had said nothing to him of these private sessions.

Jerome Brook Franklin was still with the others when Julius reached the studio. He stood panting in the doorway as the painter, frowning, straightened up from a student's easel and asked Julius with some irritation what he wanted.

—She has not been home to her mother, sir!

—Who has not? Oh. Then I expect she has gone off on some business of her own.

—Without telling her mother?

Brook Franklin knew the ways of artists'

models. He laid a meaty hand on Julius' trembling shoulder.

—I shall be twenty minutes more here, he said, and told Julius he could wait for him, if he wished to.

Julius wasted no time, when twenty minutes later he had the painter's undivided attention.

—Did she say nothing to you, sir?

—Of what?

—Of any scheme, or plan?

They were sitting in the empty studio. The dust danced in the autumn sunshine streaming down through the skylights overhead. The stuck window was now open. Brook Franklin was filling a pipe with tobacco. Shreds of black shag hung from the edge of the bowl. He shook his head, his eyes on the bowl.

—I fear the worst, said Julius darkly.

The painter gave out a short choke of laughter as he set a taper to the tobacco. Julius turned on him.

—You think it's funny? he cried.

—My dear man, said Brook Franklin, girls are like young horses, did nobody tell you that? Skittish. She has gone off on a whim. Perhaps she has a friend.

He stopped here. He was bored now, and

careless. He understood that Julius was her friend. He did not want to inflame the boy further. He wanted to get rid of him. But Julius had become suspicious.

—Why didn't she tell me about her private sessions with you?

At this Brook Franklin colored beneath his beard. Again he busied himself with his pipe, which had at once gone out.

—How on earth should I know?

—What happened?

—What are you getting at, sir? I am a painter. I *painted* her. I cannot help you further. I am sorry she hasn't told you where she's gone but I can shed no light on the matter.

—She didn't tell her mother either.

Brook Franklin threw his hands in the air.

—I know nothing of the mother!

At this Julius leaned close to him and lifting his hand, stabbed a finger at him.

—But you do. You were there. She told me.

—Weeks ago, when I wished to employ the girl. What do you accuse me of?

He was on his feet now, and growing angry. He was a stout man who reddened easily, and he stood now with his arms braced at his sides and his fists clenched. His true relationship to

Annie Kelly he was not going to disclose to Julius, and he was certainly not going to sit in his own studio and be accused of some vague malfeasance toward her—!

Julius also rose to his feet and stared at the man for several seconds, his eyes hot with tears. Then all at once he fled from the studio, banging the door behind him.

—Damn! cried the painter, and flung his pipe on the floor, where it clattered against the wall, throwing off sparks like a locomotive in the night.

I do not know where Julius went when he left Brook Franklin's studio. Somehow word got back to Waverley Place that Annie Kelly was missing and that Julius was distraught, or more than distraught, desperate, rather, out of his mind with worry. The sisters sat in their parlor wringing their hands, saying how much they wished dear Julius would return home so that they could reassure him that the girl had come to no harm; but Julius did not return home. They went in to dinner without him.

Their father was already at table casting an eye over the newspaper. He took off his spectacles and folded the paper—it was Greeley's *Tribune*—and asked Hester where her brother was. Hester cast a glance at Sarah.

—We do not know, father, she said.

—Annie Kelly is missing, said Sarah. She went out for a walk on Sunday and never came back.

Noah van Horn's head came up sharply.

—On Sunday?

He was silent through dinner, and neither of his daughters said a word. The curtains were closed and the room was warm. Cutlery tinkled on china. Plates were removed, new plates were brought. The servants moved about the dining room like ghosts, and the gas lamps flared and flickered, throwing sudden illumination upon the portrait of Noah which hung on the wall over the mantel. A nimbus of gloom seemed to surround Julius' empty chair. I can only guess what was passing through Noah's mind. Perhaps he had been expecting to hear that the girl had broken Julius' heart, and then he might predict that for a few days the boy would be disconsolate, but within a week or so would be his old self once more, having forgotten her entirely. But this sudden disappearance, what did it mean?

After dinner he retired to his library, and a little later rang for his butler, an Englishman called Quentin. Quentin was dispatched with a message and within an hour Rinder was with Noah. The two men stayed there until a late hour. Hester and Sarah heard voices raised, and crept as far up the stairs as they dared but were not able to make out what the two men were saying.

Julius returned home very late that night and everyone was in bed except Quentin, who let the boy in through the basement door. He was in a state of utter mental turmoil and unable to say where he had been. Quentin later said that as the boy drank a cup of hot chocolate at the servants' table in the basement he told the butler he had been out looking for his *mother*. Quentin, tactful fellow that he was, assumed—correctly, I believe—that Annie's disappearance had inadvertently awoken a deep sorrow of his early childhood grief and he had confused it with the death of his mother. Quentin took the sobbing boy upstairs and got him undressed and into bed without disturbing any of the family.

The next day Julius came down to breakfast in his nightshirt, wild-eyed and incoherent. He seemed to have no idea where he was, nor who his father and sisters were. He stood in the dining room beneath his father's portrait shouting that the two boats must be taken off the back of the wagon and put in the water. It made no sense to any of them, and the doctor was called. Quentin took him back up to his room, the butler being the only member of the household now to whom Julius would listen. As regards the two boats, I think that in Julius' disordered mind they represented coffins. He believed that Annie Kelly was dead, and that she would therefore require a "boat" for her last voyage. Not hard to see why he should have dreamed of boats, given his presence on South Street the previous afternoon. As for the second boat, I can only assume that he meant it for himself.

The doctor was not greatly alarmed. He sedated the boy with some opiated preparation of his own devising, then told Noah that his son was suffering from acute nervous exhaustion, the inciting agent being a sudden intense shock related to the disappearance of a young woman of whom he had become fond.

—Seem a healthy thing to you? said the doctor.

—I did not like it at all, said Noah.

—He's young. He'll get over it.

Noah gave the doctor a cigar and showed him out himself.

All that day Julius lay in his room in a state of stupor induced by the drug he had been given. His sisters sent word to Charlotte that their brother was ill. Charlotte was at Waverley Place within the hour. The three sisters embraced tenderly at the front door then hurried upstairs. Charlotte tapped at the door and without waiting marched in.

Julius was asleep. A young housemaid sat beside the bed with a basin and a damp cloth. He turned from side to side, muttering, and every few seconds cried out incoherently, and no sense could be made of any of it. The shock he had suffered was apparently being exacerbated by the medicine he had been given. Had that been all, the sisters would have drawn the same conclusion as the doctor: nervous exhaustion brought on by shock.

It was not all. The room was very warm, for a coal fire was burning and the windows had been kept closed all day; the curtains were drawn. Charlotte silently took the housemaid's place at the bedside, while Hester and Sarah stood at the foot of the bed, murmuring with sympathy as Charlotte dabbed at their brother's damp forehead.

All at once Hester uttered a scream and her hands flew to her face. Charlotte stood up and moved rapidly backwards, knocking over the chair. Sarah clutched Hester's arm and all three stared at the bed. Julius had sat up, but as far as the sisters were concerned—and they remained unshakeable on this till the end of their days—it *was not him*. They could never speak rationally about what it was they saw in Julius' bed that day—there was a *creature*, they said, and there was a smell, too, a strong smell, which they associated with raw meat and stables, and something else which they could not identify, something quite horrid—and they shrank back against the bedroom door where they clung together, open-mouthed. Apparently their brother, or whatever it was he had turned into, then began *chanting* at them, blasphemy and obscenity!

—Julius! screamed Charlotte.

The sound of his own name seems to have penetrated the boy's inflamed brain, for the fit—if that is what it was—passed off as suddenly as it came. He fell back on his pillows in a dead faint, and when Charlotte cautiously approached the bed he was fast asleep. Hester pulled back the curtains and flung open the

window, and then sank sobbing onto a chair.
Julius remained asleep for several hours more.
The doctor was again summoned, and having
briefly examined the unconscious boy announced that the fever had broken just as he
had predicted it would. The doctor dismissed all
talk of a "creature," but the sisters nonetheless
insisted that what they had seen in the bed was
not their brother.

An account of all this was given to Noah
when he arrived back at Waverley Place in the
late afternoon. He was, we may imagine, greatly
disturbed, though he too gave no credence to his
daughters' conviction that *something else* had
been in Julius' bed. He looked in on the boy and
found him still sleeping. He then retired to his
library, instructing Quentin that he would not
go down for dinner, but that when a certain
gentleman called at the house later in the evening he was to be shown straight up.

It was after nine when a large man turned on
to their block from Sixth Avenue, came striding
along the street in the last of the twilight and
then up the steps to the door. Quentin at once
admitted him.

—I have come to see Noah van Horn, he
boomed.

Hester and Sarah had the parlor door slightly ajar, and listened as Quentin murmured to the stranger to please come this way. They peeped out to see the broad back ascending the stairs behind the butler, and then the library door opening at the top, and then they heard their father's voice. The library door closed and Quentin descended the stairs. The sisters stood in the hall with eager faces and silently asked— who? But the butler only lifted his hands, he did not know either.

That certain gentleman was of course Jerome Brook Franklin. It is my belief that Noah's intention was to give him a good cigar and tell him, man to man, that Annie Kelly was no good for his boy and had been paid to go away. I see Noah with a glass of brandy, his slippered feet crossed on the head of the grizzly, his eyes on the ceiling as he then speaks of the tour of Europe he intends to make when his son is a little older. He perhaps hints that a tutor will be required for Julius, a man of sound artistic judgment and a knowledge of European art both ancient and modern—and here he casts a keen glance at his guest, knowing, I suppose, that it has always been in the nature of artists to seek patronage, and having found it to cling to it for dear life, for patronage *means* dear life to a man who wishes only to paint pictures all day— and in this way he hopes to *acquire* Jerome Brook Franklin, just as he was accustomed to acquire shipments of cotton or parcels of land or any other commodity to which he took a fancy. And why? Because if questions were to be raised about Annie Kelly's disappearance, he had to have the painter in the fold.

The door to the library was on a landing one flight up from the hall. An hour later, as Noah emerged with the painter and prepared to descend—I assume a mutually satisfactory agreement had been reached—a bedroom door opened on the floor above. The wall lamps were giving out only a low, flickering flame as the two men paused murmuring at the top of the stairs.

All at once something was flying down upon them and neither man had time properly to understand what was happening. Then my grandfather was tumbling down the stairs, and Noah was shouting, and Quentin ran up from the basement as Hester and Sarah spilled out of their parlor and screamed to see their brother, or the thing he had become, rather— the thing in the bed—stabbing at a portly man in a loud suit as they struggled violently on the hall floor. Quentin managed to pull him off and hold him back as Jerome Brook Franklin crawled away on his hands and knees with blood and jelly streaming from his face. Held tight in the embrace of the butler, Julius, his face distorted, unrecognizable—bestial!—sobbed and panted, and then began to *chant*, clutching aloft the instrument of his enemy's enucleation; I believe it was a palette knife. With it he had taken out my grandfather's eye.

I need not weary you with what occurred in the immediate aftermath. The doctor was called yet again, for the third time in two days. Charlotte arrived soon after, with Rinder, who took control of the situation. He had to; for the first time in his life Noah was unable to act. He aged ten years that night at least, in fact I believe Noah van Horn that night began to die. As for my grandfather, his wound was treated by the best surgeons in the city but they could not save the sight of the eye.

I will hurry the thing forward now. Rinder knew what to do about Julius, he did what wealthy New York families have always done when insanity erupts and scandalous behavior ensues which has at all costs to be kept out of the press: he sent him to a private asylum, selecting, for reasons of his own, a place in the Hudson Valley a few miles north of Poughkeepsie. There Julius was put under the care of an alienist named McNiven, and when the gates closed behind him they closed upon the one member of the family who could be linked directly to Annie Kelly. For the girl's disappearance was already beginning to attract the attention of the newspapers.

The story was kept alive for a number of weeks, but it could not compete with the developing crisis in the national arena. On February 25, 1860, a few months after Julius was sent away, an obscure, ill-dressed politician from Springfield, Illinois stepped off a ferry at Cortlandt Street. Two days later he gave a speech at the Cooper Union which helped to propel him into the White House, and the United States into civil war. It was a war which Julius would miss in its entirety.

For twenty years Julius remained in the asylum upstate. He received regular visits from his sisters but only one from his father. It occurred a year before Noah's death. I believe he wanted to tell Julius the truth about Annie Kelly's disappearance before it was too late.

They sat on a bench at the back of the main buildings and looked toward the setting sun over forested mountains cleft by deep-shadowed valleys. Julius was in his mid-twenties now. It was the era of what was called the moral treatment of insanity, this being an approach which stressed the exercise of constant kindness in a carefully selected location where not only the character of the carers but also the buildings themselves tended to regulate and make tranquil the lunatic mind, and lead it gently back to reason. Routine and occupation were considered essential, and activities such as basket-weaving and hymn-writing were encouraged, though in Julius' case landscape painting in oils was the chosen therapeutic occupation. But to quote the bard, you may as well forbid the sea to obey the moon as shake "the fabric of his folly, whose foundation/ Is piled upon his faith."

It soon became apparent to his father that Julius had invested his faith in a bizarre crime perpetrated by my grandfather. Julius believed Jerome Brook Franklin had built a secret room beneath the floorboards of his studio where Annie Kelly was being held against her will, forced to live on flour cakes and water in which he cleaned his paintbrushes and copiously urinated. When his students left for the day he would lift a trapdoor beneath the platform and descend to the narrow room where Annie lay in chains, and there he ravished her body for hours and nobody heard her screams but he, Julius, who alone was sensitive to the vibrating telegraphic currents in the atmosphere generated by the suffering of the girl trapped beneath those distant floorboards.

All this Julius poured out to his father as the two sat watching the sun go down behind the mountains. Noah did not attempt to interrupt him. On being shown into the reception hall of the asylum earlier that afternoon he had at once recognized the changes wrought by madness in his son. Julius was no longer a boy, but despite the new firmness and definition of the bone structure, the faint-etched life-lines and hint of golden stubble on his cheek, nor was he a man. He seemed, rather, a husk of a man, an empty man, in large part because what he gabbled made no sense. He constantly wrung his hands, and his eyes darted about the room as though in search of some elusive flying insect. When the alienist suggested that they might like to walk in the grounds, Noah understood that Julius would be calmer out of doors. The story he then heard about Annie Kelly's captivity contained a wealth of grotesque detail, much of it concerning bodily functions and their smells. He heard it to the end, then quietly told Julius that none of it was true.

Julius appeared not to hear him. He stared out at the mountains murmuring to himself as his father quietly explained his decision to pay Annie Kelly to go away, never to see Julius again, and his entrusting the job to Rinder. He then said, slowly and gravely, that Rinder had instead had the girl murdered. He paused, while Julius continued to stare at the mountains, his lips moving but otherwise showing no reaction to what his father had said. Noah began speaking once more. For what Rinder had done, he said, he felt the most abject remorse. It could make no difference now, he said, but he wished to tell Julius the truth. Perhaps, he said, he was merely trying to ease his own conscience— Julius was entitled to think it—but he wanted him to know that there would be no easing of his conscience, not ever. Guilt and remorse had leached all joy from his life, ever since the day he discovered what Rinder had done. Noah said all this, and still Julius stared at the blackening mountains until an attendant approached and quietly told Noah that his son must come in now. Julius was led away and Noah walked out to the front gates of the asylum, where in the dusk a carriage awaited him.

It is surely an image of some pathos: poor Noah van Horn, once the master of a great commercial empire, now a broken old man, his face haggard, his heart shattered by what had befallen his son. I see him pausing there with one foot on the step of the carriage and turning for the last time to gaze upon the steep walls and towers of the asylum etched black against the evening sky, and nothing for miles around but those impenetrable mountains. He never spoke to Julius again, and a year later he was dead.

What did Julius find when they let him out in the summer of 1879? He was brought home from Grand Central Station in a hansom cab accompanied by an attendant, a stout, silent young Negro in a tightly buttoned coat and a peaked cap. The house on Waverley Place to which he returned was not as he remembered it. Only one member of the family lived there now, his sister Hester. Charlotte resided uptown in the mansion Rinder had built on Fifth Avenue, a place of such grandeur that it was considered the finest house in the city until a few months later it was eclipsed by an even grander pile boasting a more spacious ballroom and several tons more marble in the façade. Sarah, youngest of the sisters, had meanwhile nursed Jerome Brook Franklin while he recovered from the loss of his eye. Love had duly blossomed between patient and nurse, and the two were married in July, 1860.

Many of Brook Franklin's painter friends attended the wedding, men with whom he had once tramped the wilderness in search of the American Sublime. They made a curious match with the families of men from Noah's world of business and politics, who had not perhaps encountered such figures before. The two camps eyed each other warily but not without interest. The getters of money glimpsed exoticism here, and for the exotic they had a keen appetite; the artists smelt commissions. And just as well, at least for the bridegroom, for what was not said that day, not openly, was that Jerome Brook Franklin's days of wilderness painting were over. A man with one eye is no good on the side of a mountain. He is fine however in a well-appointed drawing room, and as my grandfather in top hat and eye patch walked down the aisle with my grandmother, he had in his pocket three commissions for portraits of eminent New Yorkers in the van Horn circle. They moved into a large house on West Twenty-Third Street, where the second floor was converted into a studio.

Jerome Brook Franklin applied himself conscientiously to the work of portraiture, and in time he prospered, earning an income greater by far than what he could have expected from landscape painting. But he had lost the work which had once answered every deep yearning of his painter's soul, I mean the depiction of the great natural vistas of the American wilderness. In his later years a bitter, impotent rage began to eat away at his spirit. He drank to console himself, and eventually the drink got the better of him. By the end he had lost everything.

When my mother spoke of Julius' return to New York, I remember how she would fall silent and gaze into the fireplace. I know she was thinking of the times when as a girl she visited the house on Waverley Place and met her Uncle Julius there. The house is gone now, as is my mother,

but I have photographs and so I am able to
bring to life at least in my own mind what it
might have been like, the day Julius came home.
He was a little stooped, still tall and thin, his
hair now flecked with silver but as unruly as
ever. He wore a double-breasted jacket with
broad lapels, a wide cravat with a pin in it
and a narrow collar at least ten years out of
date. Across his vest hung a silver fob. He wore
wool trousers with a narrow pinstripe and laced
boots. All this is in the photograph. He carried a
bamboo cane, and someone had put a flower in
his buttonhole.

Also apparent in the photograph is a faint
reminder of what he had lost. The long, mild
face with the watery pale-blue eyes and delicate
claw of nose—a fine narrow ridge of bone under
skin as taut as parchment, I have that nose
myself!—carries the unmistakable mark of his
vanished youth. He had of course been spared
the many horrors which others had endured in
his absence, I mean not only the war but the
draft riots of July, 1863 when for days New
York was under the control of a howling mob
and all the family trembled for their lives. He
missed it all.

This, then, the man innocent of history who

came back to his sister Hester in the summer of 1879 and tentatively mounted the steps of his childhood home. The windows of the upper floors were shuttered, all but those of his old bedroom. No attempt had been made to render the façade fashionable with granite pillars or other such additions, and with its flaking columns the house now seemed dowdy and forlorn, haunted almost. When the front door opened and Hester appeared from the gloom within, Quentin hovered somewhere behind her, and behind him, in deep shadow at the back of the hall, the one housemaid who remained, Mary, who as a girl had sat at Julius' bedside in the first hours of his nervous breakdown. Hester stood quietly beaming, her hands clasped before her, as her brother ascended the steps and kissed her unlined forehead.

—Dear sister, he murmured.

—Come in, Julius, she said, and wiped her cheek.

But before he crossed the threshold Julius turned and regarded the street, cocking his head to the sounds of wheels rattling over cobblestones and the rumble of the avenue beyond, where elevated trains now clattered uptown, spewing cinders and hot coals on the sidewalk below. With a troubled expression clouding his features he lifted a hand and with one finger tapped at the air as though he were attempting to summon the word which might express an idea only dimly formulated in his mind. But no, it escaped him, and he turned indoors.

By all accounts he was grateful to discover that the house was unchanged since he had left it. Few of the rooms were used now, Hester living very quietly, eating in the kitchen with the servants and using the parlor only when one of her sisters paid her a call. Is it possible that Julius heard in the empty rooms the laughter of his childhood, when his sisters were all at home and his father still alive? He went into the library and sat silent for many minutes in his father's armchair.

Hester had prepared his old room for him. This was wise, for with evidence of change in the city streets all around him, when he retired upstairs he could at least feel himself in familiar surroundings. In the evening the lamps were lit and I imagine they dined early as had been the custom when they were young, though whether they still dressed for dinner I do not know. Perhaps since the death of Noah the old formalities had been abandoned, but somehow I suspect that for this one night, the occasion of her brother's homecoming, Hester might have felt compelled to exhume an evening gown and discovered that despite the odor of mothballs and a light coating of dust, the garment still fit her slight frame. She had then brought out her jewelry boxes, and rediscovered rings and necklaces and other such pieces whose luster, unlike the gown's, had not dimmed in the years of their neglect. And so, before a cloudy mirror, Julius' sister made herself presentable for his homecoming dinner.

I see them next in the parlor preparing to go through to the dining room. Julius is elegant in formal evening clothes, the tailcoat and high collar, and a diamond pin in his tie. Hester, bedecked with old jewels and less than comfortable, sits nervously smiling as her brother wanders about the parlor, attempting but failing to discover a conversational tone to suit the occasion. She is relieved when Quentin announces that dinner is served.

A little later, as the soup was removed and the duck carried in, she murmured a word to Quentin regarding one of the cats, and Julius came to life.

—There are cats in the house? he said.

Had he not seen them earlier? Hester glanced at the butler. The odor of camphor drifted from her person.

—There are, brother Julius.

—How many?

—Nine.

Julius was sitting straight up in his chair now and his eyes were bright.

—This is very good! he said.

—Julius, said Hester, and her tone was grave.

—Hester!

—There is something we must discuss. The others.

Julius' mood at once changed. The mild elation disappeared. His face became occluded. He said nothing.

—They wish to see you.

Still he said nothing.

—What am I to tell them, Julius?

—Who wishes it?

—Rinder wishes it. He is much changed, brother! And Charlotte, of course.

Julius pondered this. His fingers played upon the tablecloth, restlessly pleating the fabric. He watched his struggling sister from under lowered brows.

—Sarah too, said Hester. And Mr. Brook Franklin.

This name she spoke with evident apprehension. Julius did not respond.

—Very well, sister, he said at last, lifting his head and smiling at her. There was light in his eyes once more, although Hester was unsure what it signified. But her relief was great.

I believe Julius began to explore the city the next day. The Negro attendant, before leaving the house the previous afternoon, had advised Hester that in the early days, at least, her brother should always be accompanied by a member of the household when he went out. But Hester did not object when he announced his intention after breakfast of going for a walk. He asked her had she any suggestions what direction he might take.

—Fifth Avenue, she replied at once.

—Fifth Avenue, said Julius.

—Yes, said Hester, and then you can tell me what it is like.

It was decided that they should dine with Rinder and Charlotte early the following week, and I have no doubt that Hester anticipated the event with no little apprehension. Julius however seemed unconcerned. This worried Hester all the more, for she understood as well as her sisters did what was involved. Julius had not yet spoken to any of them about the events of twenty years before, and had given no clue as to how he thought of them now. He was about to dine with the man whom he had once believed to be responsible for the murder of Annie Kelly, and whose eye he had gouged out in a savage attack. Also present would be the man his father had told him was the true author of Annie Kelly's death.

Charlotte was now a stout, colorful woman and very much a character in New York society. Her opinions remained radical—she had embraced socialism—and she compounded her eccentricity with ostentatious jewelry and cosmetics, often appearing in public in flowing capes and scarves, a cigarette holder permanently in her gaily beringed fingers, loud and fearless as only the very wealthy can be. She had visited Julius in Waverley Place and gently questioned him about the coming dinner, which she had initiated in the belief that her brother must be brought back into the family as quickly as possible. She had been relieved to find him apparently sane. She had witnessed distressing scenes in the Catskills asylum over the years, and at times had thought that he would never be well enough to come home. But her fears now seemed unfounded. She considered he had made a full recovery, and wished to do all she could for him. Charlotte was deeply uneasy about her own part in poor Julius' breakdown, for it had become clear to all of them during the years he was away that not one of the dozens of pictures he had painted of the mountains had any artistic merit whatsoever. So she had been quite wrong about his genius. He did not possess it.

Hester and Julius took a cab to the Rinder house on the appointed night, and if Julius was impressed by what his brother-in-law had built on the profits of the business founded by his father, he did not say so. They were greeted at the door by an English butler a half-century younger than Quentin and shown into a richly appointed drawing room where their hostess awaited them, also Sarah and her husband—my grandfather—wearing a glossy black eye patch. There was satin and gold on the walls, an immense chandelier, little couches and marble tables, and many fine pictures. Julius paused in the doorway and stared at Jerome Brook Franklin, who stood with his back to the fire. There was a moment of charged silence—a moment to which the three sisters were acutely sensitive—and then my grandfather, more portly than ever, handsome in his dinner jacket and gleaming shirtfront, his neatly trimmed beard peppered now with silver and gray, advanced across the room with his hand outstretched.

—Julius, he said.

The three women, very still, gazed at Julius. Much hung on his response to his brother-in-law's advance. He seemed frozen, uncertain—a hint of panic appeared in his face—and then he stepped forward and extended his own hand. The two men clasped hands, and my grandfather seized Julius' arm just below the elbow and gripped it tight as the handclasp lingered several seconds and each man gazed into the other's face. Ironic, I suppose, that Julius should have returned from twenty years among the very mountains which my grandfather had been denied for the best years of his working life; but nobody alluded to it that night. The prolonged handshake came to an end and the sisters fell upon the pair with cries of joy. Jerome Brook Franklin retired to his place by the fire, while Julius sank into an armchair and demurely crossed his legs.

It was only when they were going through to the dining room that Rinder appeared. Charlotte was watching Julius closely. They had not yet sat down. A door at the far end of the room opened, and Julius' eyes fixed upon it in a manner, Charlotte said later, which reminded her of a beast of prey when it catches sight of some small animal in its territory. It was not an expression she liked, for she had only once seen it in his face before, and that was the occasion of the breakdown which ushered in his madness. Then it changed. Through the door, backwards, came a servant pulling a wheelchair. The wheelchair was turned into the room and Julius saw what had become of Max Rinder in the years he had been away.

In the wheelchair lolled a shrunken man who had clearly only a few months left to live. It was difficult to recognize in this broken creature the coiled and potent figure which once had been Rinder. The bestial malice Charlotte saw in her brother's face some moments before was now replaced by a frank astonishment. She could not know it, but in Julius' mind this wasted, dying man had for many years been a monster, and about him he had entertained lurid fantasies of revenge.

I see them then at table. I know that room

well, I was often in it as a child, before they tore
the house down to make way for a department
store. It was one of those rooms so high, so
large, a table seating forty in the middle of the
polished hardwood floor, that a human being
became insignificant within it, rendered minia-
ture against the sheer scale of Rinder's wealth;
dwarfed by his money. They gathered around
the head of the vast table and Rinder now was
most tiny of all, a minuscule fragment of a man
perishing within his own delusions of opulence.
To his right sat my grandmother, and beside her
the true possessor of delusions, or so he had
been, I mean Julius; Hester sat opposite Sarah,
with Jerome Brook Franklin between her and
Charlotte. I believe there was a seventh person
in the room, that being Rinder in the years of his
supremacy after the death of Noah van Horn.
He was there in oils, a huge portrait painted by
my grandfather ten years before. The room truly
belonged to the man in the painting and not the
withered leaf, the homunculus he had become.

A strange family group, comic even, in a
morbid sort of a way, in a room dominated
by a phantom, if we think of a human spirit
preserved in oils as a phantom. At the head of
the table a syphilitic robber-baron flanked by a

one-eyed painter and a man just out of an insane asylum, this damaged trio supported by the sisters, who flung each other electric glances of wordless understanding and gave the faltering masculine energies in the room some ballast of civilized structure. Glasses were filled and emptied. Courses came and went. Julius and my grandfather ate well. Rinder was fed by his servant, and took only a few mouthfuls, which he washed down with claret. He had something important to say to Julius, this became clear, and he made no attempt to contribute to the light drift of conversation initiated and propelled by Charlotte. As he masticated and swallowed his eyes burned on Julius, and when Julius returned his brooding stare Rinder merely nodded, as though to say: Soon you will know.

Came the moment when the sisters rose to retire and Jerome Brook Franklin selected a cigar, but Rinder lifted his claw of a hand and in his hoarse, thin voice told the women not to go, for he had something to say. A glance again flickered between the sisters. Charlotte had no inkling of what was to come, this was clear, Rinder had told her nothing. When he had their undivided attention the sick man lifted his glass, in which a few drops of wine remained.

—Julius has returned to us, he whispered—
for his voice could barely rise above a whisper,
though in fact it fluted as it spoke, more hiss
than whisper.

—To Julius, he then sibilated, and the others
joined the toast. Julius seemed eager now to
speak, but even as he cleared his throat and rose
to his feet Rinder lifted a hand and begged him
to desist until he had finished. He was despe-
rately weak but the old steel was still there, and
Julius sank down again. Rinder's uplifted hand
began to tremble and he laid it flat on the
tablecloth and stared at it. The room was
now utterly silent in expectation of what he
would say.

—A misconception exists which I have fos-
tered.

More glances flitting about the table like little
birds in a conservatory, all atwitter with questions.

—It concerns Annie Kelly.

An intake of breath now, and all eyes upon
Julius. He sat frozen, blackly glaring at Rinder.
Rinder wheezed. It was not easy for him to talk,
and he was accustomed to signaling his needs
with gestures. He gestured for water, for the
claret had spilled down his chin.

—She was not murdered.

—What? cried Charlotte.

Julius continued to glare at the man as Rinder's hand once more came up and Charlotte fell silent.

—I gave your father to understand that she was. But she was not.

Jerome Brook Franklin absently turned his unlit cigar between his lips, his frowning concentration fierce upon the shriveled Rinder.

—No? said Julius.

Rinder held Julius' eye and shook his head.

—Noah could say nothing. He felt responsible.

Light began to dawn in the minds of several of those at the table. A candle spluttered in the chandelier overhead. In the street, a horse uttered a whinny and a cabman's voice cried out. A servant entered the room and was waved away. Annie Kelly was not murdered, but Rinder told Noah she was. Noah withdrew from active oversight of the House of van Horn soon after, and Rinder's reign began. Jerome Brook Franklin was nodding now. He put a flame to his cigar and produced a cloud of smoke.

Then Julius was on his feet. He had one question only.

—Where is she?

A shrug from the bony shoulders of the dying man.

—But she did not die.

—No.

Julius sat down again. He stared at Hester with his mouth open. Hester asked him if he was all right. Did he wish to leave now? For some seconds Julius said nothing, then he closed his mouth and shook his head, as though awakening from sleep.

—Alive then, he murmured.

Rinder nodded.

—She did not suffer?

—No.

At which a sort of radiance seemed to well up from somewhere deep inside Julius, his soul most likely, and it irradiated his face until in the candlelight was seen the golden glow his sisters remembered from his youth. The years fell away, and so did the last of the madness.

—Alive, he said again.

It was not at once apparent to the women how profoundly this news would affect their brother. They left Charlotte's house soon after. Rinder had been wheeled away, and whether he was gratified at the effect he had produced, whether he was morally uplifted at having emptied his freighted conscience of its secret, I do not know. If any of those present had turned at that moment from Julius to Rinder, their observations have not come down to me. What I do know is that they all clustered about Julius on the sidewalk, and in the warmth of the evening the sisters murmured their concern, Brook Franklin standing back and gazing at his brother-in-law with sober solicitude. Then Charlotte retired to her front porch and the others stepped into their carriages and clopped away down Fifth Avenue. Julius leaned back into the upholstery, and to Hester's quick glance, and the unspoken question it contained, answered that he was tired, only tired, then took her hand in his and lifting his eyes to his sister's troubled face, kissed her fingers softly. He then set her hand on the seat between them and turned to watch the grand houses go by.

I believe that in the days following Julius did attempt to discover what had become of Annie Kelly. Rinder had little enough to tell him beyond that she had been paid a handsome sum, first to leave New York and then to allow some weeks to pass before writing to her mother. I imagine that to cause such distress to her mother would have been a supreme test of the girl's resolve, her decision, I mean, to give up Julius so as to secure them a better life. If, that is, her mother actually was distressed; she was after all an actress, and I suppose it possible that she was in on the plan from the start. When Julius returned to Nassau Street, not only did he not find Mrs. Kelly, nor anyone who remembered her, he did not find her boarding-house. It had been torn down to make way for newspaper offices.

He was oddly undismayed by this. He must have realized that mother and daughter had most likely established themselves in another town far distant from New York. But it was also possible they had returned to the city after some years, perhaps having failed to find a life that gave them what they had known in Manhattan. For that reason he continued to hope that he would meet her in the streets of the city, and so he continued to search for her.

This, then, the character Julius assumed as he took up the life in New York which had been so violently interrupted twenty years before. The gentle simplicity of his monomania—for so it must be seen, his rigid habit of daily perambulation, his wandering the streets in hope of a glimpse of Annie Kelly—somehow reminded his sisters of the unclouded innocence of his younger self. But he was no longer young, and with his slow gait and unworldly air he seemed to have drifted into old age having known nothing of a middle period of manhood, those years being lost in the obscurity of the Catskills asylum. I met him several times in the last years of the century, when I was taken by my mother to the old house on Waverley Place where he continued to live with Aunt Hester.

I remember him once telling me of a memorable walk he took soon after his return to the city. He wanted to see the seaport again, he said, and I was struck by his tone as he told me this, for he spoke of it as though he were striking into wild and dangerous country. He implied that he had to rouse every ounce of courage and fortitude he possessed to undertake such an expedition. He had walked east and south, he said—and his voice was low, his eyes bright as he said it—and I was at once caught up in the adventure of it all, eager to know what perils he had met and how he had surmounted them.

The further he went, he said, the worse became the character of the streets, and he was beginning to feel distinctly afraid. The block he was on was a poor one, the tenements badly run down, windows broken and patched with newspaper, and between the buildings criss-crossed washing lines with scraps of clothing hanging from them. The people he saw, shabby, watchful men idling in doorways, grimy children and sallow, harried women, all regarded him with suspicion and hostility. Julius tipped his hat to them and passed on. He turned a corner—the day was cloudy, he said, and threatening rain—and suddenly before him, filling the sky, and rising from somewhere by the East River near the tip of the island, a monumental block of stone towering high over the rooftops, and within it two soaring arches.

He was so astonished he could not move for several minutes. So massive was the thing, dwarfing the buildings between himself and it, and dwarfing too the masts of the shipping in the river, that he could not conceive what it was. And then in the fading light he made out cables swinging down toward the river, which were then lost to sight behind the buildings, and realized it was a bridge.

I remember I cried out with pleasure.

—The Brooklyn Bridge!

Uncle Julius appeared astonished at my cleverness. How could I have known? I don't remember what I said but I have no doubt he was telling me the truth, I mean that he had really gone for a walk and come upon the bridge without any prior knowledge of its existence. I am sure Hester did not speak to him about the Brooklyn Bridge, she may not have been aware of it either.

I liked Uncle Julius, and I remember as a child I was eager to learn from my mother what it was he had *done*, to be sent to an insane asylum. At first she was evasive. She would not be drawn. She would tell me that an asylum was not a prison and that Julius was not a criminal. But she never said it with much conviction, and with the astuteness of a child I guessed that this was the story the family liked to tell itself, that he was not bad, he was sick.

—But he did *something*, didn't he, mama?— this would be my response, and I would worry at it, the question of what Uncle Julius had *done*, until my mother grew impatient and told me please to talk about something else, and if I couldn't do that then please to be quiet. Of course I did find out in the end, through sheer persistence. Nothing is more tantalizing to a child than to come into a room and have the grown-ups fall silent and then change the subject. Nothing whets a child's appetite more powerfully than the knowledge of the existence of a secret.

It became in time all I could talk about, and I suppose my mother knew she had to tell me something if only to put an end to my questions. She would sit in the gloom of our little apartment on a winter afternoon, a cat in her lap, and gaze out through dingy lace curtains onto the street, West Twenty-Third, as it happens, where she lived the last years of her life in a state of shabby gentility contemplating the glory that was once the House of van Horn. See what we have come to, Alice, she would murmur—I was just a child, and had known no other home than that apartment, but I certainly understood what nostalgia was. And unhappiness too, for often she wept. This would be around 1910, I suppose, some forty years ago. She told me that when Julius was a very young man, no more than a boy, he had informed his father that he wished to marry a certain girl, and asked for his blessing, but his father had refused. Not only did he refuse, she said, but poor Julius was prevented from ever seeing the girl again!

—But why?

To a child who from an early age had had a pronounced streak of romanticism in her, this was of course a startling revelation. But as I might have predicted, my mother at this point became vague. Apparently the girl did not come from a good family.

—So it drove him mad?

My mother was sitting by the fire, knitting, and I have a distinct memory of the clack of the knitting needles all at once stopping, and then a long silence. She gazed out at the street once more, and in the gloom the old clock on the mantel ticked on in a silence only occasionally disturbed by the muffled thunder of the subway trains running uptown under Seventh Avenue. Then she sighed, shook her head, cast a friendly glance at me where I sat by the fire with my arms wrapped round my knees, and resumed the story.

—Yes, she said at last, I suppose it did.

The clacking resumed but it was less rapid now. This meant that my mother was thinking.

—He went mad for love?

—Oh, you are all the same!

By then my mama was old beyond her years, exhausted by her unhappiness, which I now realize was as much about the disintegration of her marriage to my father as it was to the collapsed fortunes of the van Horn family. Often there would come a moment—late in the evening as I remember it, the month November, or perhaps February, for it would be raining hard outside—and she would stop in mid-sentence, up would come her head, up would come her finger, and together we would listen to the distant sound of the front door of the building banging shut.

—Your father is home, she would whisper; and the dread upon her face came of her uncertainty as to whether or not he was sober.

—That's enough! she cried; and I was sent to bed.

I had heard enough by then to elevate Uncle Julius to heroic status—to think of it, my own uncle being driven insane for *love*! But I did want the rest, and I think my mother wanted to give me the rest, though it caused her genuine distress to speak of events which to her were the first causes of the disaster which spelled the beginning of our end; I constantly feared that she would simply refuse. Just shake her head and tell me she could not go on, it was all too dreadful. So much darkness, she whispered—and not just for us! I was of course agog to know what form the darkness would take, but I knew my mama well enough not to display any impatience. She was reluctant to arouse the family history, but I believe now that the past, vale of tears though it was, so bleak and full of suffering, was still preferable to a present in which a cold, indifferent husband came home to her night after night and reminded her of just how low we had sunk. The house on Twenty-Third Street in which we had a small apartment on the third floor, hard to heat in the winter, stifling hot in the summer, and the ice-box down the hall—once we had owned the whole building!

My mother held her father responsible. She disapproved of him just as she disapproved of Aunt Charlotte, just as doubtless she would have disapproved of me had she lived to see what I became. Her tragedy, if the word is not too strong, was being born too late to enjoy the social ascent of the van Horns, but not too soon to witness our decline. Her nostalgia was touched with acid by reason of acute disappointment: fate had cheated her of her rightful status, and for this, as I say, she blamed my grandfather.

*　　*　　*

The last detail of the story I had after a conversation with him. I have said that Jerome Brook Franklin was a gruff man, and he often exaggerated that trait in order to amuse me. When my mama took me to visit my grandmother I would slip away and dart up the stairs, then tiptoe along the corridor to his studio. Often the door was slightly ajar, and from the corridor I was aware of the powerful smell of the chemicals with which he cleaned his brushes. I would see him there before his easel in the long coat he wore when he was working, a loose brown garment such as might be worn by a janitor. Always the brown coat, always the cigar, and sometimes a model, a girl, naked or loosely draped, arranged upon a platform with a broken pillar and perhaps a clump of trailing ivy. At other times some grand dignified lady with a vast bosom and hair stacked high would sit imperiously before him, and on the easel I would see her painted head, and beyond it the head itself.

My grandfather was aware of my presence even though I had made no sound at all. Without turning he would bark at me in a tone of mock annoyance.

—What is it you want, nuisance child? You

have come to distract me because the women don't want you, is that it?

But he would not turn, nor would his eyes move from their single track, the sitter and the canvas, back and forth, and the brush in his hand flickering here and there as the cigar smoke streamed from him as though he were an engine. I said nothing, merely hitched myself up onto a paint-spattered stool in the back of the studio and sat silently watching. He talked about me to his sitter.

—My daughter's child, he would say. She's a van Horn like her mother. All mad. My brother-in-law, they had to send him away! Into *my* mountains!

So it would go, and a large part of the pleasure I took from being there came of listening to my grandfather talk about the family, which he did in tones of *faux* horror, saying we were all mad. It was a good joke. After a while he would turn to change his brushes and see me perched on my stool, and pretend to be surprised.

—Are you still here, you damn little monkey? Go on, get out, get away downstairs, I've had enough of you!

Off I would go then and wander about the

house until I heard my mama calling me. Then
we would go home.

But one day my grandfather adopted a different tone. He had no sitter in his studio that
day and he seemed in good humor. There was a
bottle of red wine on the floor by his easel and a
glass of the stuff close to hand. He was putting a
few last touches to the portrait of an eminent
banker with a high bald head and a mean face.
He even hummed as he worked.

—Oh it's you again, is it? Back you come like
a case of the pox, no one will have you, will
they? Sit down over there but don't say a word.

After some minutes I forgot that I was not to
say a word.

—Grandpapa?

—What is it, worm?

—What happened to your eye?

At this he stopped working and turned to me.

—My *eye*? he growled.

He fingered his eye patch, watching me closely, and I thought he might take it off so I could
see the empty socket beneath, if that was what
lay beneath. But he did not. Instead he came
close to me and I could smell the wine and the
cigar smoke on his breath. All at once I was not
sure what sort of game we were playing. I felt a

little afraid. He put his face very close to mine, and the bristles of his beard touched my skin.

—It was your Uncle Julius, he whispered.

His breath made me feel ill. I thought I might be sick.

—Uncle Julius, I whispered.

—He attacked me, he whispered.

—No.

—Yes. I ruined his life, and he ruined mine. The girl belonged to me, you see, and it was too much for him!

I remember his laughter as I ran along the corridor and down the stairs, how it boomed from his studio and swirled about me like a cloud of cigar smoke and only grew fainter when I came panting to a halt in the drawing room, where my mama and my grandmama were having tea.

—What *is* the matter with you now? said my mama.

I could not tell her. It was too dreadful. The secret was revealed. I held it close in my heart for many years and in time I understood that mine was not the only family in which violence and insanity had erupted in generations past, and plagued the lives of those to come. They are all dead now, and what survives of them are the phantoms, merely—the daguerreotypes, the photographs, the paintings. The portrait of Noah van Horn came down to me, and as I say, I spend too much time in front of it. It all began with him, of course; it was Noah who denied Julius his chance of love, and why? Because of a prejudice acquired as a function of fear. Love must never be denied, never!—as I have cause to know, and better than most. For the story of Julius, so painstakingly assembled by means of the fading memories of those who knew him, and the ghosts now clustered on my walls and sideboards—do they not all clamor the same sad warning? That love denied will make us mad? I think so.

GROUND ZERO

Danny Silver was like a son to me, and as a childless woman who never married I do not say this lightly. He was also my patient. For seven years we had been meeting twice a week to talk through his problems, which were largely sexual in nature, and which originated in a suffocating maternal relationship which created conflicts that ran like fault lines deep in his psyche, becoming visible only when he tried to sustain intimacy with a woman. Dan was eager to enjoy a healthy relationship, but the damage had begun early, and it was structural, so progress was slow. I was not in New York when the terrorist attacks occurred, but Dan was, and the events of that day disturbed him profoundly. It became clear to me that our work would for some time be thrown off track by the repercussions of an assault which he was not alone in regarding as having been directed at himself, as in a way it was.

He was a large, sad, untidy man, highly intelligent, and his face so creased and fissured that he seemed prematurely aged, as though burdened with the weight of all of human history. I believe this had been true of him even in childhood. He dressed carelessly and had an air of constant distraction, and he did not look healthy; he took no exercise, and ate badly. He was resigned to the prospect of spending several more years in therapy, recognizing that with two wrecked marriages behind him he could not afford to make another mistake. In conversation he was given to frowns, groans, and sighs, and during our sessions together he would watch me closely from darkly bagged eyes that teemed with complicated anxieties. It may have been the very tortuousness of his mind that propelled him into a career in the law, and I believe he was a very good lawyer. Civil rights was his area.

He came to see me soon after my return to the city. We sat in my apartment on Riverside Drive one warm evening in late September. The sun was setting over the Jersey shore and the Hudson was a lovely silvery gray in the last of the light. So tranquil was the view from the window in my consulting room, with its wide western exposure, high above the river, one could almost forget the horror at the other end of the island. Dan sat down heavily, and with his elbows on his knees, and his head pushed forward, said he was a worried man. He feared for our civil liberties, he said. He feared that Congress was going to push through a bill letting federal agents lock up anyone they didn't like the look of. He said these new powers would be exercised with no judicial oversight, and the people the feds locked up would have no access to legal representation.

He rubbed his cropped skull as he voiced these troublesome thoughts, and then sat staring at the floor and shaking his head. I waited for what was really on his mind. Finally he looked up, and quietly told me that in the immediate wake of the attacks he had gotten into a situation with a woman.

—Go on, I said.

He met her the Saturday after the attacks. About forty, he said. On the small side. Black hair, good body—very intense woman, he said—little cleft chin that juts out—he jutted out his own chin, smiling slightly, absurd gesture in this big, blue-jowled man—sensitive, smart . . . Not a woman to inspire affection, he'd thought on first meeting her, too, oh—cool—for that, although at the time that had had no bearing on their relationship. He had found her through an escort agency which advertised in the back pages of *New York* magazine—

Here he paused. I was aware Dan used prostitutes, nothing new there. In fact I encouraged it.

—Go on, I said.

He was not strong, he told me, nobody who lived in the city and had been there that morning was strong. He was finding it difficult to work. It brought back everything he had suffered after his mother's death: the same disabling grief, the same leaching of joy and purpose from projects which had previously given meaning to his life. The same sudden debilitating waves of anger and wretchedness and despair. Dan lived in one of those big apartment buildings on the north side of West Twenty-Third, and it was there that he'd grown up. His mother had died in that apartment. Both his marriages had failed in that apartment. His bedroom had a balcony with a wrought iron rail and a view of downtown.

He'd heard it on NPR that morning, that a plane had gone into the World Trade Center. He'd turned on the TV and listened to the first reports, standing on his balcony high over Twenty-Third Street and watching the north tower burn.

Then he'd seen the other plane go in and with a lurch of stupefied incredulity realized that *New York was under attack*. He called his office and talked to his partner. Later he saw the south tower fall, and heard a roar like distant thunder as clouds of dense smoke billowed up from the tip of the island. For a moment, no more than that, the tower left a ghostly image of itself in the empty air. Dan remembered trying to resist the numbness he felt creeping over him by thinking of people who lived downtown, or worked there—people in his office, colleagues, friends . . . Later he watched a man he knew slightly, a man who worked for the city, come limping along the block, covered from head to foot in gray ash, and go into the apartment building on the opposite side of the street. He could see him in the lobby of the building opening his mailbox.

After a while he turned off the TV and made his way over to Union Square. There were many who shared this impulse, he said, and they milled about together, disparate New Yorkers finding what primitive comfort they could in the face of the destruction unleashed upon their city. Establishing transient bonds with strangers so as to escape the horror of solitude in the face of so much death.

Which was why, a few days later, he had called the escort service.

The woman gave him a brief firm handshake and sat down. They quickly arranged the money side of it, then she went into the bedroom and got undressed. Apparently what followed was clinical rather than passionate, which did not surprise me. She was very businesslike, said Dan, very efficient. Good cold sex. When it was over, he said, they stayed in bed, talking, and it seems that what Dan called a "rapport" sprang up between them.

—What kind of "rapport"?

She relaxed. She was interested in him. Wanted to know what he did. Had he grown up in New York? That sort of thing. She made him laugh. Dan never laughed, a sardonic bark was the closest Dan ever got to laughter, and I assumed that was what he meant. I must have said something to that effect.

—It wasn't like that, he said.

—Like what?

He was frowning. He stared at the floor, sitting forward in the chair, trying to be clear about what he meant and what he felt. He had caught the tone of my voice, my dismissive response to this "rapport" he'd achieved with a woman he'd hired for an hour.

—We connected.

—Go on.

But then it seems the mood changed. They were talking about the attacks—what else did anyone talk about?—and it became clear that she had been through something far worse than him. She was badly scared, he said. She wanted him to help her, or at least listen to her and not just write her off as a crazy person. She was an artist. She did escort work to cover the rent on her loft. She lived in a building seven blocks from the Trade Center, and from her rooftop she had watched the first plane go in. She'd heard it coming down the west side. It was very loud until just before it hit. Then everything went quiet, and she thought they'd turned off the engines. She said it went into the building as if it were going through tissue paper. The building *swallowed* it, she said. And through it all, through the impact, and the silence, and the shock, and the smoke, her only thought was of the guy who'd left her bed an hour earlier to go to work on the 104th floor.

Dan fell silent here. He wanted me to grasp the significance of what he'd just told me. I hardly needed his portentous silence to engage with the woman's experience; there were many such stories at the time and I'd heard worse.

She called the guy on his cellphone—his name was Jay, she said—and he answered on the first ring. She was close to hysteria, but his voice was calm. She could hear chaos in the background, screams, and the smashing of glass, and he told her that it was getting pretty hot and smoky in there. He asked her what had happened to them and she told him, a plane had hit the building. He knew this already, it seems he just wanted it confirmed. They had to shout to make themselves heard, but even as he grasped the enormity of his predicament he remained steady and calm, in fact *he* was comforting *her*. He told her he loved her. He told her to be happy. Then he said he had to call his father to say goodbye, and the line went dead.

From her rooftop she could see men and women clustered in open windows and out on the ledges of the high floors of the tower. She could see people falling. She said she stood there on her roof with her cellphone in her hand and stared at the burning tower, trying to make out which of those distant falling figures was her lover.

All this she told Dan in flat neutral tones, sitting forward in the bed and staring out of the window such that she gave him her profile, and he lay on his side watching her: two strangers, he remembered thinking, each seeking succor in an hour of fearful desolation, and it counted for nothing that the pretext of their meeting was commercial sex.

Still staring out of the window she began to speak again. She told Dan that later that day the cops had evacuated her from her building and she had gone to a hotel uptown. The day after, she was on the east side subway. She was thinking of her last conversation with the guy, with Jay, as the train pulled out of Grand Central. The people who'd just got off were pushing toward the turnstile, but one figure stood unmoving at the edge of the platform.

He slowly turned his head and stared at her.

She said all this in a low, quiet voice, her arms

wrapped tightly round her knees but with no
other obvious signs of distress. She hammered at
the window and ran back down the subway
car—

Dan asked her if she was sure it was him.

She looked straight at him then, and her eyes,
he said, seemed for a second or two to flare up as
though they were about to burst into flame. Then
they died once more into guardedness and opa-
city. Oh, she was sure. She had seen him quite
clearly in that brief instant before the train went
into the tunnel. She said she would never forget
the expression on his face. What was the expression on his face? Grief. Grief and pain. Grief and
pain and sorrow and loss and anger. A terrible
quiet sad anger, and it was directed not at the men
who had murdered him, but at her.

Poor Danny. Again in deep waters. A brief
rueful grin as he rubbed his skull and I gazed
at him, thinking, this poor damaged man who
loses himself in the problems of others so as to
forget his own, and now what has he done?
What has he gotten himself into now?

—Go on, I said.

She told him she spent several days in Grand
Central after that, looking for him, and it was

not difficult for me to imagine this distressed creature moving among the crowds of commuters, peering intently into the faces of hurrying men, accosting total strangers, showing them a photograph. In the immediate wake of the attacks there were many in the city who refused to give up hope, and continued to search for their lost loved ones despite overwhelming evidence that their loved ones were gone. Dan knew this, and he asked her what she thought the guy— Jay—would have said to her, if she'd found him in Grand Central. She'd leaned toward him, he said, a hand spread on the pillow and the bedsheet slipping from her breasts—and it broke his heart, he said, her reply.

—I don't know. But he hates me now.

She saw the plane go into the tower and she didn't do anything to save him. What could she have done? Nothing, of course, but what aroused Dan's pity was that she felt responsible for his death. And he understood that the dead man, or her projection of him, rather, this— what?—ghost?—did not merely materialize on the periphery of her consciousness, but that he was capable of states of feeling which directly affected her. He had agency.

* * *

I have been in clinical practice in New York for many years, and I have encountered this before. In fact it is not uncommon, the conviction that one is being reproached by a loved one who has recently died. It is a function of unresolved guilt, and in acute cases there may be features of psychosis, as apparently there were here. I could have tidied her up in a couple of sessions, no great problem there, routine psychiatry; but as regards Danny, who was, after all, my primary concern, the situation was a little more complicated. He had observed the suffering of a woman he had hired for sex, and been affected by it—by her distress, I mean, at having seen what she took to be the ghost of her dead lover in a subway station in midtown Manhattan. He had been asked for sympathy and he had given it; he had been able to help a creature more vulnerable and needy than himself, and this was the source of the "rapport." This is what gave him the feeling of connection. It was a flimsy foundation upon which to build.

—Dan, did she "work" while she was seeing this man?

—I don't know. Does it matter?

*　　*　　*

Does it matter. I said nothing. We sat there in silence. I made a note of this last interchange; it told me much. I was then struck by the idea of Dan hiring an escort for an hour, then having to employ his psychiatrist for a further hour to help him make sense of the experience; he was nothing if not mediated! He then told me he awoke on the Monday morning profoundly depressed. That would be September 17. He had been thinking about her all weekend. Another of those clear cloudless days, the sky deep blue, and a fierce Atlantic light seemed to bleach to utter naked clarity every building and every face he saw on the street. He walked to his law office, which was on Broadway just below Canal. In midtown it was all bustle and jostle, traffic snorting and fuming, a seemingly normal day in New York: people going to work, getting on with their lives, emphatically not prostrate with shock and grief; we New Yorkers are a tough breed, resilient, but the further south he got the more unreal the city became. There were soldiers in the streets, and cops everywhere. National Guardsmen. Emergency vehicles, road blocks, searches. Smoke was rising from the fallen towers and the air smelled very bad. Many people were wearing face masks, which compounded the air of sur-reality.

His waiting room was crowded with unhappy people. Dan and his partner were working *pro bono* for downtown residents needing help with legal problems arising from the attacks. The first to come into his office was a woman who lived in Battery Park and wanted to make funeral arrangements for the husband she'd lost. She wanted closure, she said, for her children and for herself. But how could she have a funeral when she didn't have a body? Then she wept, she wept uncontrollably, and Dan had to come round from the other side of the desk and comfort her. He worked without a break and by eight that evening he was exhausted. He had eaten nothing but a bagel all day. He thought he was done. He had already poured himself a second glass of wine, and put his feet up on the desk, when there came a tap on the door. Wearily he crossed the room and opened the door. It was her. The prostitute.

She was as surprised as he was. They stood uncertainly in the doorway for a moment, then he brought her into the office and closed the door. She lifted her hands to his face and he was at once strongly aroused. At the same time he wanted to tell her that he would have to refer her to his partner, but her touch was like an electric current, he said, and certain structures of inhibition in him had been weakened by fatigue, by stress, by the wine he had drunk, and now with the woman's fingers on his face he knew what was about to happen and did nothing to prevent it happening but accepted the inevitability of its happening and relinquished all responsibility. There was nothing clinical about it this time, rather the swift certain passion of two adults eager for physical penetration without delay. That is how it happened, as he described it to me, there on the couch in his office, her with her skirt hauled up to her hips, and him with his trousers at his knees, and tenderness played no part in it at all. But this time, he said, it wasn't cold.

He gave me his slightly canine expression here, wary and tentative but at the same time pleased with himself. Sexual guilt and sexual evasion had done much to exacerbate his problems with his mother. Encouraging him to talk frankly about his sex life seemed to help.

—Go on, I said.

When it was over she sat up on the couch and, with her back to him, straightened her skirt.

Then without a word she crossed the floor and disappeared into his bathroom.

Later they opened another bottle of wine. Not wise for a man with an empty stomach and no real head for alcohol, and I said this to him. I said I was concerned now. He seemed to have launched himself on a reckless trajectory with this woman, and he admitted that was true. Then there was the ethical side of the thing, and this troubled him considerably. They did talk about her legal difficulties, he said, all the ash and dust in her loft, the expense of living in a hotel and the landlord demanding full payment of rent even though she couldn't get back into the building, all of which he said he could help her with.

—You were trying to move the relationship onto a professional footing, I said.

Dan looked sheepish. Not exactly. They went back to his apartment and he persuaded her to stay the night. He thought he was falling in love. He thought it was a kind of breakthrough for him.

I let this pass in silence. They did sleep for a few hours. In the morning—another of those beautiful clear days which seemed to mock us that fall, when obscurity, fogs, rainstorms even, would have given the city some relief from the hard edges of an unbearable physical reality—she wrapped herself in his robe and went out onto the balcony where he had stood watching the towers burn. He heard her cry out.

—What is it? he shouted.

He leaped from the bed and found her staring down at the street. She turned to him, her fingers spread across her mouth.

—He must have been down there all night, she whispered.

—Who?

—*Him*. Jay.

And then, said Dan, he felt as though he had crashed to earth. All at once he became leaden and weary and bored. He could see only the empty street, and the empty sky where the towers ought to have been. It depressed him horribly, that empty sky.

—Nothing there, he said, in what she later told him was a tone of indifference.

—Oh Dan, I murmured.

I had heard this story, or variations on it, from him before. It was the old terror. He had not changed. It was how he drove them all away in the end. He had been unable to suppress the spurt of bad faith—quelled in an instant, but a real event, nonetheless—and the woman had recognized it even as she turned away in distress from whatever it was she had seen in the street below. He'd watched the door close behind her and the self-disgust had compounded inside him—

Now he sat in my living room as the night came on, and his big shoulders heaved in the shadows. I stopped him here. I had only one question for him.

—Do you want me to see her, Daniel? Don't answer now. Think about it.

The big man got up out of his chair and I walked him to the elevator. As the doors closed his eyes were on me, and his face was full of questions. I nodded, I smiled, I wanted to reassure him. But I was not at all happy about this relationship. He thought he was falling in love, and he may have been right, but he was falling in love with a prostitute. This was not appropriate for a man who, in emotional terms, was only just beginning to learn to walk. I needed to see her.

Later that evening I wrote up my notes of the session. I wrote that so destructive had been the impact of the terror attacks on Dan's psyche, they had in effect pushed him back to a more primitive stage of libidinal organization. Not only was he buying sex, he was buying a kind of spurious emotional intimacy with a woman who was more damaged than himself, and mistaking the comfort it gave him for love—a woman, in addition, who lived so close to the Trade Center she had seen the people falling, and been traumatized by the experience. I had not yet visited Ground Zero, but it seemed I could postpone it no longer.

I went down that night, late, not wishing to be among a crowd of ghouls. I had the cab driver take Seventh Avenue to Varick. We were stopped at Canal by a soldier who questioned me before allowing us to proceed. For several blocks the streets were dark and empty. I got out at Worth and at once smelled an acrid, smoky odor, the source of which had been apparent for the last few minutes I'd been riding in the cab. To the south the night was lit with powerful artificial light, a pale, milky blue in color and framed by high buildings which boxed it in and gave the impression of a film set on a night shoot. Smoke was billowing up through this weird light, and I could see cranes moving about.

I went south on West Broadway, which was deserted. All at once a group of men in hardhats emerged from out of the smoke, steamfitters or welders, or engineers perhaps, tramping up out of the smoking horror covered in dust and ash. They looked exhausted. I walked east on Chambers then, badly shaken, but determined to get as close as I could. I saw the circling lights of emergency vehicles, I heard sirens and also the steady background hum of heavy generators. There was another sound too, a steady rumbling and clanking and rattling, the sound of demolition and clearance, giant backhoes and diesel excavators with huge shovels and hydraulic arms grappling debris and loading it into trucks: the big diggers.

I reached Broadway and headed south toward the site. Across from City Hall the phone company was digging up the street. A sanitation truck went by, its yellow lights blinking, spraying water to keep down the dust. More barriers, the familiar NYPD trestles, painted blue, stencilled, familiar from a thousand street closures of one kind or another. Cops manned the barriers and talked to what few visitors were still about at this late hour. Not far from the Brooklyn Bridge I came level with the ruins. All that had once been familiar was strange to me now, and it was not easy to know what I was looking at. Down a side street—was it Fulton, or John?—I saw a high building torn open, its innards sheared off and spilling out, twisted beyond recognition and starkly illuminated by that unearthly blue light; at the sight of it I was viscerally awoken to the magnitude of the violence that had occurred here. When the towers came down, corkscrewing as they collapsed on themselves, they spewed out steel girders which tore open the walls of adjacent structures, and what I saw now was physical evidence of forces of an almost unimaginable destructive power.

At Liberty Street, sick to my soul, I could go no further. I stood behind a police barrier among a small silent crowd and stared at what remained of the south tower. I saw in the glare of the floodlights fretted sections of the tower thrusting up from mountainous piles of smoking rubble, skewed from the true like tombstones in the nearby graveyard of Trinity Church. These monumental shards of the towers' aluminum-faced columns with their slender gothic arches were all that remained standing, and I felt as though I were gazing at the wreckage of some vast modernist cathedral.

The destruction reeked of hatred and evil, and it reeked, too, quite literally, of death. I am a psychiatrist. I do not believe in evil, I believe all human experience can be traced to the impress of prior events upon the mind—

But this. As I began to walk back uptown I attempted to find a few sticks of thought with which to build a structure that might explain why those men had done what they had to us. To *us*. But I could not, and all at once I felt what was, for me, a most rare emotion, I felt *rage*— the sort of blind primitive destructive rage which I imagine drove those men to attack us as they did.

Dan and I met again four days later, on October 3. It had not been easy for any of us. There had been no more terror attacks, but New York's suffering was now compounded with the fear of biological assault. It seemed our water supply was susceptible to deliberate contamination, in fact there were rumors that it had already been poisoned, with the result that many people in the city, myself included, were drinking only bottled water now. The Bush people claimed they were working to strengthen our "biodefenses," and smallpox vaccine was being stockpiled, some forty million doses of it. Who would be the lucky forty million, one wondered. We were not reassured to learn that our doctors were not trained to recognize the symptoms of smallpox, botulism, or bubonic plague, although they were getting better at identifying anthrax, as we now had at least two confirmed cases in Florida, one fatal. So to the various psychic afflictions that had come in the wake of the attacks, by which I mean feelings of dread and anxiety, nightmares, flashbacks, sleep disturbances—catastrophe sex and delusions of love—were now added paranoia and terror. And we were at war. There were troops on the ground in Afghanistan.

We talked about all this. Dan mentioned the feeling of raw incredulity that would often take him by surprise, these strange days of late September and early October—can this be reality? reality in America?—as though, he said, glimpsing suddenly through the window of a spacecraft a world utterly alien, utterly different from the world he had come from; but then found his thoughts returning, unable to concentrate on what his city and his country had become, to the equally bewildering state of his own heart: the fact that he was falling in

love with a woman he didn't begin to understand.

—No, I said, that's what you need me for.

In the flush and flood of his newfound happiness he gave me one of his rare grins, his face
splitting open in a ramshackle fashion such that
half of it was squeezed and creased by the side of
his mouth that went upwards, the other half
pulled taut by the side that went down. It was
comical and endearing, and I thought: he is, at
this moment, a child. At this moment he has
regained the childish aspect of his nature. As
though he had never been scarred and calloused
and hardened, not at the deeper levels. But I
knew that this flood of shallow feeling was only
masking his damage, and that what he was
experiencing was just the brief elation of a false
liberation from phobic structures very securely
embedded by his mother.

But I said nothing of this. I asked him to tell
me what happened next. After he'd driven her
away with his indifference.

He called her hotel several times, he said. He
always left a message but she never returned his
calls. When he finally went to the hotel, to wait
for her there, all night if necessary, he was told

she had gone home. He told the receptionist he was her attorney and produced his card. He said he had to reach her urgently, so she gave out the address.

—You were prepared to sit there all night? I said.

—Yes.

—What if she'd been working?

—I didn't care. I had to see her.

This I had never known in Dan before. He had never tried to find his way *back* to a woman, once he'd felt the impulse to flee. The next day he left his office at six and walked west across Tribeca to Duane Square. The dull roar of heavy machinery clanked and rattled from Ground Zero. A truck rolled by with buckled sections of steel girder lashed to it. He found her building and pushed the buzzer. It took what seemed a very long time for her to respond.

—Who is it?

—It's me. Dan.

—I'm coming down.

There was a loud click and he pushed open the heavy industrial door. A bleak hallway with walls painted gray, a rack of mailboxes. To his left the rusty metal gate of a freight elevator.

Dan could hear it slowly descending, the oddly terrible sounds of shivering metal and screaming cables. Then she was hauling open the heavy gate and he stepped in. The operating lever was made of brass and seemed to have come straight out of a Hudson River tugboat. As they clanked back up to the top of the building the woman stood stony-faced in the big dusty cage and Dan said nothing, thinking: at least I am in. Her T-shirt and jeans were smeared with ash. Her hair was tied up in a red scarf, and the sweat was streaming down her face. A smudged face mask hung round her neck on a thin elastic band. She was filthy, and—because of it, he said—more desirable to him than ever. After a silent eternity the elevator shuddered to a halt and she hauled the gate open and went through into the loft.

All the furniture had been pushed up to one end so that she could scrub the floor and walls. At the other end, beyond the area cleared of furniture, a door stood open, and he saw an easel with a tall narrow canvas clamped to it. It too had a thick layer of ash. The windows over the street were open but the air in the loft was heavy with a fine-grained dust. White motes drifted through slanting beams of light in the warm evening sunshine. The smell from Ground

Zero was foul, and Dan wondered what exactly he was inhaling. She stood by the door and stared at him, and he stared back, and there was, he said, a profound wordless connection; and then she was in his arms. He knew it was going to be all right. When finally they broke apart she set her hands on his shoulders and regarded him with fond amusement.

—Do you want a drink?

He asked her what she was having and she said gin and tonic. He asked for the same. He watched her at the counter as she sliced a lemon. The snick of the knife on the cutting board. Then all at once, as though she had heard her name being called, she lifted her head and put down the knife and stared at the window. Dan said that for some reason he thought of a body of water, a sudden gust of wind, clouds passing across the sun—she was always somehow elemental to him. She turned to him then. Her face was pale. She bit her knuckle. Her eyes filled with tears.

—I'm so frightened.

He held her gaze.

—Will you help me?

—I'll try.

*　　*　　*

He paused. Dan had a habit, when he gathered his thoughts, of making a steeple of his fingers and resting his forehead on it. I had begun to think this woman he claimed he loved was borderline schizoid, certainly there had been enough psychotic breaks to justify that tentative diagnosis. What she said to him now left me in no doubt at all.

—You remember the morning the towers came down, you remember thinking, this is not real but I'm seeing it?

—Yeah.

—That's what's happening to me all the time now. He's not real, but I'm seeing him.

He is not real but I am seeing him: what a wealth of pathology lay buried in those nine words!

—Dan, I said—and this was something I had been reluctant to press him on before, but now I felt I must—Dan, don't you think I ought to see her?

But he cut me off at once. It was out of the question. He had already suggested it to her, and she had said no. He was adamant. I had been afraid of this.

—Then let me take a look at her at least. In a café or wherever. Some public place.

—Why?

—I need to see her face, Dan. We talk about her, I form impressions from what you tell me about her, but it's hard to know what I'm dealing with.

—I'm dealing with her, he said, and I could see how uneasy he was with the idea of secret surveillance; this was a man, after all, who had made a career out of civil rights abuses. But deeper even than that, I realized, there was something else: there was the fact that he was afraid of her.

—She won't find out, I said.

—She might.

—And then?

But this was not to be contemplated. A shake of the head. Nothing more to be said. Very well, I would say nothing either. So, a stalemate. But we had known each other a long time. Now I did apply pressure.

—Daniel, I said, employing a certain tone of voice with which he was familiar. A short pause ensued.

—All right! Oh Christ. There's a place on West Broadway, near the subway.

He told me the name of the restaurant. He said he met her there for coffee in the morning if he could get away from the office.

And so the next day I found myself once again within a few blocks of Ground Zero. The sky was clear, the air temperate, a lovely day—any other October. But again I smelled the foul acrid reek from the ruins, which now seemed to me less harmful to the lungs than it was to the soul, for it carried with it emanations of the evil which had created it in the first place. There were firemen in the streets of Tribeca and also in the restaurant, a trendy place with a zinc bar and a dining room in back, and a few tables up front under a mirrored wall where the specials were written up in what looked like lipstick. The firemen sat eating large breakfasts: workers from the site ate for free in all the downtown restaurants; there'd been a piece about it in the *Times*. They would have been out of place—any other October. I sat down and ordered a coffee. A few minutes later the firemen left. It was 10.40 and still no sign of them. I decided to wait until 11.

At five of they came in. She was smaller than I had imagined her, though otherwise she fitted Dan's description. But he had never mentioned what I should have thought a rather significant characteristic of the woman: she was Chinese. Or Asian, anyway. Not beautiful, but certainly feline, the small heart-shaped face under a slick helmet of black hair, as if she'd just stepped out of the shower. She carried herself with a certain arrogance, and there was cruelty there too, something hard and dark; she was like a black stone, a little chunk of polished jet. She wore a black T-shirt under a denim jacket, and a short black skirt. She was slender, assured, flawless of feature and complexion, and as the waiter emerged from behind the bar with menus she flounced past him without even a flicker of acknowledgment. I realized I did not know her name.

He followed her into the restaurant displaying great discomfort. He glanced at me and he seemed, in the company of that petite slinking creature, more bear than man. His hair was uncombed. His black leather jacket looked shapeless, almost sack-like over his humped shoulders, his rolling gait. I thought absurdly of a man unsteady on the deck of a ship in heavy seas. She glanced at herself in the mirror, and by means of the mirror on the opposite wall I saw her properly for the first time, and knew what she was. They went into the back, and I could still see her in the mirror. Dan was fingering the menu and talking to her, and she sat beside him on the banquette picking delicately among the contents of a small leather purse. Only once did I see her lift her face to his, and caught a gleam of animation in those black-cat eyes.

It was when they were leaving that I got what I'd come for. She paused at my table.

—So now you know what the crazy woman looks like, she said, or sneered, rather.

I was cool. A small bewildered shrug.

—I'm sorry?

I tipped my spectacles down my nose as I gazed up into her vicious little face. I saw how very angry she was, close to hysteria.

—Why can't you just leave me alone!

Then she turned to the hapless Daniel.

—You stupid fuck, she cried.

She swept on out of the restaurant, him scurrying after her without a single glance of reproach. No manifestation of anger at all.

That came later. By god he was furious. How could I have done it? More to the point, how could he have let me do it? It was a total fiasco. A debacle. She was far too smart not to have known she was being scrutinized by a stranger, and having seen it to then realize that Dan was implicated—what an idiot he was! But I was not

interested in his histrionics. What was the upshot, I wanted to know. The upshot? Ha! Fierce,
baleful glance from eyes hot with rage. The
upshot. The upshot was, he'd spent practically
the rest of the day attempting to make her listen
to him.

—Listen to what, exactly?

He became all at once defensive. He said
something inaudible.

—Daniel?

—To my apologies! he cried. My abject fucking groveling apologies! You didn't come out of
it so well either.

This last he muttered darkly, as though it was
at least some consolation to him that in his
general debasement he had blackened my character in her eyes. I told him that didn't matter.

—It may not matter to you.

—Dan, you didn't tell me she was Chinese.
What's her name?

—You realize you've never asked me her
name until now? She's called Kim Lee. And
she's as American as you or me though I
shouldn't have thought that needed saying!

And I suddenly saw the extent to which he
was in thrall to the woman, to this *Kim Lee*.
He had crossed the line that separates patho-

logical obsession from healthy sexual love, and her displeasure had cast him into a state of terror—terror of loss, of abandonment, of solitude—and I could only imagine the things he must have said and done to mollify her. Did he not see how deftly he was being manipulated? She had refused to allow him into her building. She would not pick up the phone when he'd called her from the street. He had hung about in Duane Square when he should have been at work, miserable, angry, jealous— ironic, this, given that she was already haunted by one lover who gazed up at her window from the sidewalk.

I interrupted him here. I had had quite enough of his tantrum.

—Who are you jealous of, Dan, her other clients?

—Her other clients, he said bitterly. Then: She doesn't do that anymore.

—Oh she doesn't. Who then?

But he would give me no more, and his refusal was remarkable for its stridency—almost, I might have said, its passion. But what I did learn from his outburst was that something had happened before he'd met the woman, something to do with the guy who'd died in the attacks, this Jay, and that there was more to it than guilt.

Later, when he'd gone, I found myself more troubled by his state of mind than I had been before the encounter in the restaurant. He'd told me that Kim Lee didn't want him to talk to me about her, in fact she didn't want him to have anything more to do with me. Apparently she thought me evil, and said that I wanted only to destroy their relationship. She had come as close to weeping as he'd ever seen her. Then she had pleaded with him, saying that if he abandoned her she would surely be lost. She needed him. Nor was it difficult to imagine the physical blandishments that would have accompanied this performance. I could see her in his broad lap, her fingers all over him, her face mere inches from his own, her black eyes gazing helplessly into his as she shifted her little Chinese hooker's body about in his lap—no, not difficult to see where that conversation went!

So it was to Dan's credit that he did not obey her, but came to see me anyway. He made clear the risk he ran, for if she found out—and now I knew, he said, how little escaped her—she would never see him again, and about that she had apparently been adamant, and Daniel believed her; this time he knew she meant it.

I didn't believe she meant anything of the sort. It was not yet clear to me what she wanted of him, and perhaps it was not clear to her either, but of one thing I was now certain: she would not let him go, now that she'd got her claws in him. And something else disturbed me, which was my suspicion, or conviction, rather, that Dan was holding something back. It was connected to the remark he had let slip concerning his jealousy, and then the defensiveness with which he'd refused to elaborate. Who was he jealous of? Surely not the dead lover. That would be tantamount to feeling jealous of a *ghost*, and while this is well within the normal range of human sexuality I felt there was more to it than that. There was something obscure, just out of sight, somewhere in the recent past; and I felt I had to identify it.

I stayed up late that night, and only got to sleep around five in the morning, with nothing resolved in my mind.

The bombing continues in Afghanistan while in America we are under bioterrorist attack. Already eight people have been diagnosed with inhalation anthrax and three of them are dead. It comes in the mail, or so it was thought until a woman who did not handle mail professionally fell ill, and now fights for her life in the intensive care unit of a Manhattan hospital; the source of the anthrax deep in her lungs is unknown. The government warns us that another terrorist attack is anticipated and that we should be at a heightened state of alert. But alert to what? We are told no more than that.

Episodes of peripheral insanity have erupted, random bits of evil apparently stimulated by the attacks, as for example the deaths aboard a Greyhound bus in Tennessee, when a knife-wielding Croatian slashed the driver's throat and the bus careered across two lanes of on-coming traffic, then flipped over, killing six. There is an Arab man in custody who enlisted in a Minnesota flying school and aroused suspicion when he expressed a desire to learn to fly large commercial jets but apparently showed no interest in taking off or landing. This sort of thing we deal with every day now. I read my newspaper; New Yorkers speak out: "Nothing feels normal." "My life is ruined." "The world is over." Dan tells me what John Ashcroft's people are up to, the ethnic profiling, the round-ing up of as many men as they can find of Near Eastern or North African descent. The suspension of due process, the wholesale pullback of traditional American freedoms—

I do not tell him this but I am beginning to think that John Ashcroft is right.

Daniel by this point was pathologically obsessed with his Chinese prostitute, and I saw how difficult it would be to get him to talk about what had happened before he met her; that is, before September 11, a date which was rapidly becoming a watershed in all our lives, a line of demarcation, or a point in time, rather, before which the world seemed to glow with a patina of innocence and clarity and health. And after which everything seemed dark and tortured and incomprehensible, bearing nothing but portents of a greater darkness to come. It was against this black and shifting backdrop that Dan's affair with the woman was playing out, and I was forcibly reminded of an image that I had once seen of two actors engaged in a furiously complicated drama in front of a screen on which were projected enormous indistinct shadow-figures performing obscure destructive actions which mirrored and at the same time grotesquely distorted the drama going forward center stage. What I wanted from Dan was that larger perspective.

I called him the day after his last visit but he wasn't home. Nor was he in his office. I didn't leave a message, but continued to call him every hour until at last I got him, by which time it was late in the evening.

What followed was one of the most trying conversations I ever had with him. At once I heard the resistance in his voice, his unwillingness even to speak to me on the phone, so seriously alarmed had he been by Kim Lee's demand that he have nothing more to do with me. For some minutes he was curt and circumspect, and I had to become rather crisp with him. Did he or did he not need my help? Was I to assume he wanted me to break off the therapy and leave him to flounder unaided in the quagmire of delusion in which he now found himself? Did he want to go it alone?

There was, I could hear it, an impulse in him to cry out—Yes! Yes! I want to go it alone—I don't care what happens to me—I don't care if I sink, let me just fling myself in, go under with no thought of consequences, careless of the damage I do to myself—but we both recognized the infantilism of the impulse. A kind of suicidal infantilism, a primal unthinking embrace of the death instinct, this is what I heard awoken in him as I spelled out the alternatives he faced, and the implicit ultimatum they contained. He did not give voice to the impulse. There is in the end this at least to be said for a training in the law, that a kind of professional filter effectively screens one's drives, one's emotions—one's delusions—so that one does not become entirely the slave of pathological forces originating in the unconscious mind. I knew my man. I knew what those forces looked like as they manifested in him at the time, fuelled and propelled as they were by an intense sexual intoxication. He could not abandon me: to abandon me would be to cast himself adrift upon towering seas with no raft, no lifejacket even save his own confused and fragile psyche. He could not do it. Insanity even to contemplate it, though contemplate it he did.

—What is it we have to talk about? he said wearily.

I told him we had to talk about the man who died in the north tower, and in the same weary tone he said he supposed I was right. I told him we should do it now, and again he agreed, and I was surprised to discover there was no resistance left in him at all. But when I asked him would he come here, or should I come to him, he replied with more alacrity and affect than I'd had from him in a long time that good Christ no, he couldn't have me in his apartment; he would come to me, of course he would.

—Then I'll see you in a while.

I put down the phone with the feeling that I still had the situation under control. But there could be no relaxation of vigilance. I felt as though I was engaged in terminal conflict with the prostitute Kim Lee, and the prize was Danny Silver's sanity.

We were in my apartment and I had told him that I was sure he was withholding information from me, and I asked him how he expected me to help him if I did not know what was going on. I was quite severe with him. I saw his big hand smear across his face, smear the leathery folds of stubbled flesh—he had removed his spectacles—then rub his skull as his eyes drifted unseeing into some, to me, inaccessible place in his mind. He sat forward and stared at the floor, a big, blunt-fingered hand still rubbing at the crown of his skull, his elbows planted squarely on his knees, and his feet set wide apart on the carpet, the whole a monument to solidity although there was nothing solid there at all. With the compressed precision of a mind trained in the law he gave me the facts of the case.

The affair with Jay began in June, he said. Summer of 2001, three months before he, Dan, had met her, so all he knew about it was what she had told him; and as to the reliability of *that* information I was naturally skeptical. But I did not say this, I told him to go on, for I felt I would be able to at least pick out the bare bones of the thing and superimpose my own interpretive construction. And I was confident that my interpretation would be closer by far to the reality of the events he described than whatever meaning that woman imputed to them.

She'd described to Dan how she'd picked up this good-looking guy at a gallery opening in Chelsea. Jay Minkoff was his name, and he was apparently the son of a prominent New York banker and philanthropist. The details were scanty and it was not, I imagined, an episode Dan was anxious to know much about, given his own feelings for Kim Lee; but he surprised me. He began to grow animated, and I realized that so emotionally invested in the woman had he become that he spoke about her experience with the same intensity he might have employed to speak about her skin, or her breasts, or the sound of her voice; and the fact that it concerned her previous lover mattered not at all. What mattered was that it was *hers*. So it was giving him vicarious pleasure, this—what?—refracted nostalgia, speaking of the emotional life of the woman he loved even though they were the emotions she had felt for another man.

—He was a rich kid, kind of preppy, and she didn't really like guys like that but all the same he was the sort of guy she felt she could trust. A very sweet guy. And he was very good at intimacy. She thinks intimacy is what we want. It's the best part of love. Or maybe passion is the best part of love. Is it passion or intimacy?

—Just tell the story, Daniel.

He *was* learning fast. But this was not my Dan. I heard the Chinese prostitute in every word he uttered. He went on with the story. She was apparently brazen in her approach to him. She told him in the middle of a crowded art opening that she was taking him home to show him her artwork. He said he'd like to see her artwork. She'd like to show it to him, she said, showing her work gave her almost as much pleasure as sex.

So then he asked her if she was always so direct, and she told him she'd reached an age when it made no sense to be anything other than direct. What age was that, he'd asked her, and she'd told him how old she was, so now at least they had that out of the way. She was sixteen years older than him. They didn't waste any time because there was so much what she called "bed in the air." They left the opening and cabbed downtown.

Bed was—satisfactory, said Kim Lee, in response to Dan's wary inquiry. Jay had to leave early in the morning to go to work, and she didn't know if she would ever see him again. He traded in futures, apparently. Futures.

Dan shook his head at this sad irony.

—You seem fond of the guy, I said.

—I never met him!

—I know. Go on.

It appears that after Kim Lee's initial rather lazy and entirely physical response to this sweet man with his high-powered job in a brokerage firm, and his interest in art, the relationship turned serious.

A slight falter here. A new charge of feeling in Dan's tone. Again the steepled fingers, the frown, the few seconds of silence as he gathered his thoughts.

—She fell in love with him? I said.

He was silent. This was difficult for him. More kneading of his forehead with his fingers.

—Not at first.

But later she did. Hard to know precisely when it happened. Another pause. She was annoyed with herself, he said, but at the same time curious to see if the machinery—this was her word—still worked. And pleased that she had not grown so jaded that falling in love had ceased to be a possibility.

Why was she annoyed with herself?

She said it was so much work. She knew what would happen, she knew she would fall hard, she always did. Then she smothered them and they ran away. That's the problem with men, she'd told Dan, not that you're faithless, though you are, but that you buckle.

—We buckle? he'd said.

Poor Dan. He had buckled often, he was seriously structurally flawed, and I believe she was aware of it. I didn't pursue it then; instead I asked him to try and explain what he had observed of Kim Lee's capacity for love. When he was ready to answer me he said there was a kind of—ferocity—in her which he had occasionally seen roused, and when that happened she could be as passionate and possessive as any woman he had ever known—hadn't she said that she smothered her lovers and then they ran away? And that pattern—men she loved running away—had taught her caution and detachment: all this she had explained to him, apparently, whereas he, Dan, he said, had always believed that falling in love involved the idealization of the other. Kim Lee was incapable of that, he said, but she was more than capable of fighting for her man like a tiger, and giving herself sexually such that after one night with her, any man—

He stopped here, all at once aware of how fatuous he sounded. I said nothing; I just watched him shake his head in mild self-disgust, and rub his big hand across his skull.

—Like a fucking teenager, he muttered.

I decided to be easy on him, at least for a little while. I knew the sort of woman Kim Lee was, about her true nature I had never had any doubts at all. This detachment Dan spoke of, it would of course be an essential component of her personality structure, given that the woman largely supported herself by prostitution. Hard to imagine, though I did not say this to Daniel, that a prostitute could ever idealize a man. A woman who sold her body would most certainly have mastered a capacity for detachment, and would clearly see—if she didn't anaesthetize herself—what it was she was doing, and what it was she was dealing with—that is, men. She would become as astute a judge of men as one was likely to find. Whores and psychiatrists—who sees clearer the true shapes and shades of men?

So for such a woman to fall in love after a few nights of casual sex, this was an idea I regarded with some skepticism. What I saw, rather, was enlightened self-interest, the American way. She was an American, or so Dan claimed, and this was the American way. She knew, of course, about the guy's family, she knew who his father was, and I said this to Dan. But he did not properly take it in, he was thinking about what came next; and it was in the course of those subsequent revelations that I discovered what it was exactly that he'd been keeping from me, and just how sinister were the circumstances surrounding Kim Lee's affair with Jay Minkoff.

*   *   *

It was late August, and they'd been to a party at the Guggenheim uptown. The evening was warm. They'd wandered aimlessly for a few blocks, and he told her he'd grown up in the neighborhood. He showed her a townhouse just off Fifth. They stood on the sidewalk then suddenly he stepped forward and pressed the bell.

They were shown into his father's study. A tall sleek man of sixty rose from his desk. He was wearing a cashmere cardigan, corduroy trousers, and brown suede shoes—she seemed to have fixed in memory every detail of the encounter—and greeted them with pleasure. His name was Paul Minkoff. Kim Lee had met men like this before, senior Americans accustomed to the exercise of power and possessed of a mannered charm that could shift in a moment to implacable iron authority. They sat in leather armchairs and drank good Scotch from a well-stocked liquor cabinet. The room was lined with books. There were paintings on the wall which she recognized. She was deftly interrogated about the art she made, and it was evident that nothing she said provoked the older man's interest. What did provoke his interest, however, was the woman herself. She saw it in the way he looked at her, the tone of voice in which he conversed with her. And he knew she saw it, she told Dan, he intended that she see it, this subtle compliment he paid her, the oblique wordless suggestion he was making. I asked Dan if the son saw it too.

—Not until they were leaving.

—What happened when they were leaving?

—He gave her his card. He'd mentioned a gallery on Fifty-Seventh Street, he'd given them business in the past. If she wanted an introduction he'd be only too happy, that sort of thing. They both knew it wasn't going to happen.

—What?

—That she would be of any interest to that gallery.

—So what was the card all about?

—Exactly.

—And Jay?

—He said his father never gave his card out like that.

I thought: the older man who feels he must behave with a kind of sexual gallantry toward his son's woman so as to demonstrate his potency. Compete in an arena where he suspects his powers might soon fail. Establish dominance.

—She kept the card?

—Yes.

—Why?

This was more difficult. A long pause. I grew a little impatient. This older man, the father of her lover—what were her feelings about him? A snort of scorn from Dan here.

—If she had any, he said.

If she had any. I remember how he said it, how it burst out of him, as though it had been trapped under pressure for some time. It made a strong impression on me. I was encouraged. It said much about the nature of his infatuation with Kim Lee. If she had any. I thought I might at last be making progress. And I thought: he is at least honest enough to recognize that the woman is cold and selfish, even if the insight makes not the slightest impact on his own state of besotted enthralment. It perhaps even intensifies it. The fact that she was in some fundamental way inaccessible to him, this only sharpened his already acute desire for her. I knew I was about to cause him pain.

—So who started it?

Up came his head. His eyes were wild, the eyes of a man stumbling out of the wilderness after days of being lost.

—Daniel? I said.

—He did. Of course.

—Go on.

He called her. Apparently he told her that he had better see for himself what her art looked like, if he was going to help her. Dan said wearily that they both knew what he was saying. And what had been Kim Lee's response to this proposition? Dan stared at me, and there was more of wonder than horror in his voice as he articulated the full implication of that one brief seemingly innocent, altruistic phone call. The suggestion that he come see her art.

—It excited her.

—She told you that?

Dan said that she lived at a pitch of such equilibrium—curious choice of word, I thought, for the emotional emptiness of a sociopath—of such equilibrium, he said again, laying emphasis on the "such"—that a jag like that—

—Like what?

—The idea of fucking the father, he said, as the bitterness and contempt again erupted and then was swallowed—it excited her. And he had never seen her excited by an idea. Only by physical sensation.

We sat in silence pondering this. A fire truck

went south on the West Side Highway, its siren wailing and its horn bellowing. Another dead fireman had been recovered at the site.

—Where were you when she told you this?

They were at her place. It was night. She was by the window, talking to him about the Mink-offs, father and son, her eyes on the street below. Dan was weirdly hypnotized by what she was saying. Then at a certain point she came over to him, stepped across the shadowy room, and bending low over his chair, and leaning on her hands on the arms of the chair, brought her face close to his so he was at once conscious of her fragrance; and the desire which was always active in him when he was with her grew suddenly urgent. She breathed a few words in his ear and laid her fingers on his groin. Again they wasted no time, not even to get to her bed. It happened there in the armchair and involved no more preparation than the unzippering of his fly and some small adjustments of underwear—

Dan did not understand the dynamic, how sexual arousal could be brought on by this perverse story of imminent seduction. When they were done she turned on some lights and made them each a fresh drink, then sat with him in the armchair, curled up like a cat on his big body. Not once, said Dan, did he feel the impulse to pull back, nor at the time was he troubled by the dark turn in her narrative, the admission, I mean, that she was entertaining the possibility of having sex with the father of the man with whom she'd claimed to be in love. Later Dan told me he came to feel deeply disturbed by what he regarded as a kind of moral failure in himself but at the time he'd felt fascinated, and yes, excited.

She told him she tended to avoid men like Paul Minkoff but at the same time the fact of their power attracted her. Dan asked what her experience of such men had been but she dismissed the question with an elliptical reference to collectors, and the uptown dinner parties she occasionally had to attend; and besides, she said, her own father was no different.

A rich seam, this, I thought, but not immediately relevant.

—Do you hate her for it?

Quick immediate shake of the head. No, he didn't hate her for it. I didn't believe him. It may be a cliché that love, or certain states of love, rather, are close to hate, or are hate in another register, but it is a cliché because it is true. He did hate her, and what he said next convinced me of it. He said that when she told him about Paul Minkoff's phone call he'd seen what he called her "real self." He said she defined herself to him in that momentary gleam of excitement, that sudden light in the eye, the small wicked smile and glimpse of white teeth—that was who she was. She stood revealed. A woman who could take pleasure in the admission that she was excited at the prospect of betraying her lover with his own father.

—Hardly surprising she's haunted by the poor bastard, he said, can you imagine the level of guilt?

We were back to guilt. I had not yet addressed the issue of guilt. To my mind this was pedestrian psychology. It was too easy, too obvious an interpretation of what the woman was all about. It satisfied Dan, but then he lacked the detachment required to think imaginatively about her. He saw Kim Lee rocked to her foundations by a ghost, and thought of guilt. I was not so sure anymore.

—Go on, I said.

He went on. And this was where the pain came. What she had told him, and what he had supplied from his own jealous and obsessive imagination I did not trouble to separate out, but it does not matter. Paul Minkoff was with Kim Lee within an hour of the phone call. He came to the loft on Duane Square, and what a sophisticated game they must have played. She showed him her art. They kept a distance from one another, but less of a distance than if the encounter had been innocent. They did not talk about Jay. This simple conversational omission would have given her particular pleasure, I believe—the not-talking about Jay. How long had they danced this dance, her bringing out her small canvases, her small exquisite drawings, laying them on the table, and him standing beside her to examine the work she showed him, not touching her, not even brushing against her bare arm, but the pair of them acutely aware of their physical proximity and fiercely alert to the knowledge of the far closer proximity implied by his very presence in her loft—and I knew that Dan was experiencing this state of almost intolerable sexual tension at one remove as though it were he, Dan, who had stood next to Kim Lee at the table, almost as though he were remembering the first time he had met her, and known, even as he brought her into his apartment and they arranged the "money side" of it, that this woman would in a short space of time be in his own bed naked. It was hard not to be affected by his projection of self into an imagined scene of slow certain mutual seduction.

Suddenly he threw up his hands, threw himself back in the chair and shook his head like a dog shaking off water.

Another of our silences. I allowed it to expand. This was the source of the jealousy he had alluded to. And I realized then why he had acquiesced in this sordid story, or even, as he himself said, become complicit in it by not expressing his moral disgust—it was because he was taking pleasure in his own torment. There was a masochistic element here which had not escaped me. Daniel was a man who since the death of his mother had lived in a state of emotional numbness, and we had talked about it often, the anxiety he experienced because he could not seem to *feel* anything anymore. He was certainly feeling something now, and I realized that in a certain way it was immaterial what it was.

—So they had sex, he said. That's all.

—And afterwards? I said quietly.

He was pacing now. For a second or two he

bit at his thumbnail. This was hurting him. I knew it would, but I wasn't going to let him off yet.

—Christ, must we?

—Yes.

And he glowered at me then, he gave me the face of thunder, all blackness and rage and misery! He was a powerful man, a man of strong passions, and he was hurting to his core. But I wouldn't let him off the hook. He stood at the window with his back to me and spoke to the glass.

—Afterwards.

—Yes.

—He paid her.

Of course. It was of a piece with the whole tenor of their transaction, or transgression, rather. The cold and loveless nature of what they had done, the implicit cruelty of their behavior. It was not simple lust that brought them together, it was far darker than that. Of course he paid her. That was part of the game, that he should treat her as a whore, his son's lover. But at what point does one say—this is evil? I am a psychiatrist. For my entire professional life, until, that is, I went down to Ground Zero, I had rejected the concept of evil. I had believed only in the impress of bad circumstances on the vulnerable mind. Not anymore. And now, hearing Dan's account of two adults taking pleasure from a third party's ignorance of their actions, a third party with whom they were both on terms of intimacy, and whose knowledge of those actions would prove utterly devastating—for them to run this risk, and for one reason only, their own pleasure—was this not evil? I am inclined to think it was.

But it hardly mattered now. The potential for devastation had been established, and it was, in a way, out of all their hands as to whether this devastation would actually occur or not. Whether they would get clear of it, all three, without harm done, without damage to the innocent. He paid her, and she took the money. It was a sophisticated game, there was a *veneer* to it. He paid her and he left. Dan blew air out of his lungs and sat down heavily in the chair.

—Just like you did, I said.

I watched him extremely carefully here. But he was not shocked, nor angered, that I had drawn the parallel between himself and Paul Minkoff. He had seen it himself.

—Just like I did.

Another silence. The big man was letting go
of it now, he was unburdening himself, and he
must not be hurried. There was much I still
needed to know, but I was in no great hurry to
find it out. It had already occurred to me that
Jay Minkoff eventually discovered the truth
about Kim Lee and his father, for Daniel
seemed to be shaping his narrative so that it
pointed toward just this kind of a denouement.
I wanted to resist this tendency. I wanted not to
be swept along on the current of Dan's account
of events. I suppose what I wanted was quite
simply to keep an open mind for as long as I
could. Guilt, both emotional and forensic, was
central to his account, and in regard to the
latter—the moral responsibility for an evil action, I mean—I did not want to be rushed. So I
suggested that we break off our conversation
for a day or two.

But he was not happy with this idea. He
wanted to discharge the full awful burden of
the thing and he made this very clear. I saw his
frustration and his annoyance. There were
groans and sighs, rubbings of face and skull.
Then he returned to his original question, the
question that had brought him to my apartment
on Riverside Drive late at night and against his

better judgment, and the tone of voice was one of utter bafflement and perplexity.

—So why did she do it?

—Why do you think she did it?

I had known even before Dan arrived at my apartment that night that if I could bring him this far then much might be accomplished. I had made him tell me how she was put together, this beguiling, dangerous creature, and he had answered me thoughtfully and frankly. I had led him from there into the affair with Jay Minkoff. Now the question: what *else* was there in Kim Lee, that she would behave as she had with the guy's father? I gave him time to think.

—Because she's the devil.

Inwardly I exulted. He may have barked with bitter irony as he said it, but that was not the point. He was turning.

—Go on.

—Christ, I don't know! Because there's that thing in her we all have, that drive or whatever you want to call it to work against our own interest. The self-destructive urge. To tear down whatever we've managed to build, whatever's good.

—And where does that come from?

—You want me to say the death instinct but I

don't believe in the fucking death instinct. Maybe she just wanted to have sex with him and thought she could get away with it.

—She could have had sex with anyone. She did.

He fell silent. Again I said nothing. I had brought him face-to-face with an aspect of Kim Lee he had deferred confronting until now. I had no great confidence that an epiphany was about to occur; insight is never a guarantor of behavioral change. At least let him see her clearly, this devil who'd infatuated him so utterly, at least let him define the element in her nature he had so far avoided or denied.

But he was allowing me no access to his thoughts.

—All right, I said, let's talk about what happened next. Paul Minkoff comes down to her loft, ostensibly to look at her art, and they have sex. Then what?

He stared at the ceiling, and the lamp on the table beside him, the only light I had lit in the room, threw his face into a wild terrain of chasms and gullies: he was all pain. The big dome of the forehead was scored and slashed with his suffering.

—He paid her and he left.

—Did they make another appointment?

—I guess so. It didn't end there.

—They established a pattern. A structure to the thing.

—Yeah. The kid went to work and an hour later the old man showed up.

Oh, and the bitterness, the hollowness of the laugh that accompanied that bald statement of fact—!

—Then one day they got caught, I said.

—Yeah.

—You think they wanted to get caught?

He was at the end of his tether. He would have given up at this point, stood up, stormed out, whatever—but he didn't. I wouldn't have let him, and he knew it.

—Did they want to get caught? I guess they must have. It's very sick.

—They both wanted it?

—I guess he was as sick as her.

—Why?

—He knew the risk they were running.

—But where did his sickness come from?

—He must have hated his son. I don't know why. You tell me.

—Why do fathers hate their sons?

He grew fractionally less hostile when I made a

question general, moved away however minimally from the fraught local specifics of the thing.

—They're threatened by them. They arouse the fear of death in them. They resent a potential which no longer exists for them. I don't know the fucking man!

—Do you think she's still having sex with him?

Again I had pushed him to the edge. I saw him struggle with it. I could not know exactly how deep his true feelings were for the Chinese prostitute. It was possible he would throw in his hand, shake his head and walk away. As far as I was concerned that would be the best outcome of all. But if he refused to let go of her—

Again he would not reveal his thoughts to me. Enough that I had forced him this far.

—Alright. So they got caught. What happened, Jay came by the loft one morning and found his father there?

—Something like that.

—Go on.

So he told me what he knew. They were in bed, Kim Lee and the old man. They heard the buzzer. They might have ignored it, but Jay had a key. She buzzed him in. The elevator opened directly into the loft so the old man had nowhere to go. He stayed in the bedroom. Kim Lee was at the door in her robe when Jay stepped out of the elevator. She made him coffee.

Listening to Dan narrate all this in a flat, tired voice, step by weary step, I could not help but be suddenly urgently engaged by the scene he described. I imagined in Kim Lee an excitement of which she revealed nothing, as she moved around in her kitchen in her robe, making coffee for her lover. She had never been more alive than she was at that moment, in that state of exquisite tension, with so much hanging on what happened in the next few minutes, and Jay languidly murmuring to her, unaware that his world was about to be devastated.

The tension was too much for the old man, apparently. Growing bored of hiding in the bedroom—he had never in his life had to hide from anything, power exempts one from having to *hide*—he stepped into the kitchen. The astonishment of the son.

—Daddy! What are you doing here?

The silence that follows. The stillness. The three figures frozen in space as they await the sickening impact of whatever it is that is coming at them at unimaginable speed—

*   *   *

Ground Zero has now shrunk to the extent that I can stay within two or three blocks of the ruins on all but the west side of the site. As I thread my way along narrow streets that once lay obscured in the shadow of the towers, new perspectives are suddenly apparent. That gothic remnant of the south tower, five stories high, is now visible in its entirety from the stub end of Greenwich Street just off Rector. Beyond it, from high pipes, water pours ceaselessly into the ruins, where subterranean fires still burn, and smoke lazily drifts up among the tilting cranes into a cloudless October sky.

Last week on Broadway, close to Wall Street, I came upon a store that I had never noticed before. It is called THE NEW YORK STOCKING EXCHANGE. It used to sell underwear of a sexually provocative variety; patronized by the likes of Kim Lee, I imagine. Behind a metal grille the plate glass of the store window has cracked, and large shards of glass lie among the disordered display. A limbless, headless mannikin's torso clad in a skimpy red teddy dangles from a string, turning gently in the breeze. The legs of mannikins thrown down by the blast and still sheathed in fishnet are covered in thick gray

ash. And there is a large sign that reads: 20%
OFF ALL BRAS AND GIRDLES.

Bush has signed the Patriot Act, much to the
disgust of those who believe it gives federal
authorities powers far beyond anything concei-
vably necessary for our national security. That
is not all. Ashcroft has pushed through a change
in prison regulations which will allow federal
agents to listen in on defendants' conversations
with their lawyers. This sounds to many people
like an egregious violation of the attorney-client
privilege, and it's been said that the Justice
Department is becoming insatiable in its desire
to destroy the Bill of Rights. I would have said
the same myself, once. Not now. Not after what
I've seen. But Dan and I have not talked about
any of this, in fact Dan and I have not spoken
face-to-face since the night he told me about
Kim Lee's betrayal of her lover, and their subsequent reconciliation: it seems Jay Minkoff in
effect *refused to absorb* the pain his father
attempted to cause him, and decided instead
to try to understand the impulse behind the
injury. Then he went back to Kim Lee to salvage
their relationship.

—It was the last act of his life, Dan had said.
Probably the best.

I'd been frankly skeptical. It may or may not have been the last, best act of Jay Minkoff's life, but I was certain of one thing: the prostitute Kim Lee did not deserve such generosity. I said this to Dan. He lifted his big head and fastened his weary gaze on me. For several seconds he silently stared at me, and I began to grow distinctly uncomfortable. Then he spoke.

—I don't think you're much use to me anymore, he said.

We have had a number of telephone conversations, but he is adamant: he wishes to discontinue his therapy. He says he does not need me. This is a worry. He is not strong. He may have succeeded in the short term in suppressing his terrors but they have not disappeared. They will come back, and when they do he will run away, convinced that Kim Lee is suffocating him, just as his mother suffocated him when she was alive; then he will need me. In our last phone conversation he told me he was moving in with her. I asked him if he thought this was wise. What would happen to the apartment on Twenty-Third Street? Surely he'd be keeping it, in case everything went wrong with Kim Lee? But no, he was selling it. He said it was full of ghosts.

Battery Park City is open again, though strange in its emptiness, the absence of the usual convoys of strollers and nannies, joggers and roller-bladers. The apartment buildings in this affluent development at the southern tip of the island suffered extensive damage when the towers came down, and a number of moving vans are in evidence as tenants, perhaps with small children, and worried about air quality, head out for the suburbs. There is an esplanade along the Hudson here, and very peaceful it is on a fresh autumn day. Many of the workers from Ground Zero eat their lunch here, gazing out across the river at the large construction projects clearly visible on the Jersey shore, these in stark contrast to the grisly demolition going forward on the Manhattan side.

I saw them once. They were coming out of a restaurant on Greenwich Street. They didn't see me, or at least I don't think they did. They gave no sign. He shambled along beside her, and at one point threw an arm around her narrow little shoulders. They looked happy enough. I miss my big bear but I think he will come back to me when the affair collapses. He knows I am here for him, I don't have to tell him that. For now, just to catch the occasional glimpse of him is enough. I wonder what he's doing. I wonder about the woman from Battery Park, the one who wanted a funeral for her husband but had no body to put in the coffin. I would like to know if he got her a funeral. Did she find closure? Did she, Dan?

A NOTE ON THE TYPE

The text of this book is set in Linotype Sabon,
named after the type founder, Jacques Sabon. It
was designed by Jan Tschichold and jointly
developed by Linotype, Monotype and Stempel,
in response to a need for a typeface to be available
in identical form for mechanical hot metal
composition and hand composition using foundry
type. Tschichold based his design for Sabon
roman on a fount engraved by Garamond, and
Sabon italic on a fount by Granjon. It was first used
in 1966 and has proved an enduring modern
classic.